DEATH UNDER THE SUN

ADAM CROFT

BLACK CANNON
PUBLISHING

First published in Great Britain in 2014.

This edition published in 2021 by Black Cannon Publishing.

ISBN: 978-1-912599-73-8

A CIP catalogue record for this book is available from the British
Library.

Printed and bound in Great Britain by Clays Ltd, Elcograf S.p.A.

MORE BOOKS BY ADAM CROFT

RUTLAND CRIME SERIES

KNIGHT & CULVERHOUSE CRIME THRILLERS

PSYCHOLOGICAL THRILLERS

- Her Last Tomorrow
- Only The Truth
- In Her Image
- Tell Me I'm Wrong
- The Perfect Lie
- Closer To You

KEMPSTON HARDWICK MYSTERIES

1. Exit Stage Left
2. The Westerlea House Mystery
3. Death Under the Sun
4. The Thirteenth Room
5. The Wrong Man

All titles are available to order from all good book shops.

Signed and personalised books available at
adamcroft.net/shop

EBOOK-ONLY SHORT STORIES

- Gone
- The Harder They Fall
- Love You To Death
- The Defender

To find out more, visit adamcroft.net

It had never occurred to Ellis Flint to put the lid back on the bottle before shaking it, and he cursed his momentary lapse of concentration as he scraped tomato ketchup from the Artex ceiling with a palette knife. Mrs Flint would never have made a mistake like this. Though Mrs Flint was, of course, hopelessly at work.

The ringing of the doorbell jolted Ellis, causing the palette knife to jab into the ceiling and a lump of ketchuppy plaster to plop gracefully into one of the mugs of freshly-brewed coffee that adorned the kitchen table.

Alighting the wooden chair, Ellis made his way

carefully across the laminate flooring and towards the front door, careful to avoid getting ketchup on his socks. Kempston Hardwick was, of course, expectedly early. And Ellis Flint was expectedly late.

Hardwick smiled as he greeted Ellis, who noted the distinct lack of ketchup stains on Hardwick's immaculate clothing.

'I've made you a coffee,' Ellis said, gesturing for his friend to sit at the table as he spooned the customary six sugars into his own mug.

'Of sorts, yes,' Hardwick said, his nostrils flaring as the bitter steam assaulted his olfactory system.

'I know you've always been telling me I should get some decent coffee in, like the stuff you make at home, so I did. Trying this Nescafé stuff now.'

'Yes, well I was thinking perhaps something a little less... granulated.'

'Come off it!' Ellis said, stirring his own coffee as he plonked himself down on the wooden chair. 'You've seen the adverts. It's the same coffee, just in granules.'

'I haven't, actually,' said Hardwick, who didn't even own a television. 'And that wouldn't really go any way to explaining why it's half the price and a tenth of the taste, would it?'

'Do you need to be so snobbish about everything?' Ellis asked, his head bowed slightly at what he saw as a personal affront.

'There's a big difference between being snobbish and having standards, Ellis. I am not a snob; I just have higher standards than most.'

'If you ask me, it's all down to stress.'

'Stress?' Hardwick asked, one eyebrow raised.

'Yeah, it's in this book I've been reading,' Ellis replied as he leaned over to grab an almost pristine paperback from the kitchen dresser and plonked it on the table in front of Hardwick. 'It says that stress is the silent killer. Usually, other people are the first ones to notice that the stressed person is behaving a little oddly.'

'I see. And you think I've been "behaving a little oddly", do you?'

'Well, no. Sort of. Actually, I don't know what would be considered odd for you, Kempston, but de-stressing never hurt anyone, did it?' The resultant silence would've been obvious enough to anyone else to have signalled Hardwick's disagreement, but Ellis Flint was not just anyone else. So he continued. 'I've been thinking, actually.'

Hardwick made an uncomfortable grunting noise, seemingly at the thought of another worrying brain-wave from Ellis Flint. 'Go on...' he said as he eyed the suspicious reddish-white blob floating in his coffee mug.

'Well, like I said, you've had a tough time of it lately, haven't you?'

'No I haven't.'

'Personally, I'd call two murder investigations pretty damned tough,' Ellis insisted, referring to the previous cases on which they'd worked over the past couple of years. The first, the murder of former light-entertainer Charlie Sparks, had given them the cause to meet and become friends. The second, a case involving the murders of three residents in the sleepy market town of Tollinghill, had been particularly taxing.

'Personally, I'd call it my duty to have investigated them,' Hardwick replied. 'Besides which, I fail to see what you're getting at.'

'Well, I just thought you might need a holiday. That's all.'

'A holiday?'

'Yes, Kempston, a holiday. You know, going away somewhere and enjoying yourself. Not moping about Tollinghill waiting for people to die.'

'I do not mope, Ellis,' Hardwick replied. 'Nor do I wait for people to die. If people have the unfortunate habit of dying within my general proximity, I'm rather at a loss to do anything about it.'

Ellis Flint took a sip of his coffee, himself rather at a loss to do anything, having been once again bamboozled by Hardwick's characteristic way with words.

'Anyway, I think a holiday would be a good idea,' he finally said.

'And I don't.'

'But why not? The prices are very good this time of year, for starters. John Tyler's in Shafford have some great deals on at the moment. I saw one deal to Egypt, a fortnight in an all-inclusive resort complex, for just—'

Hardwick's coffee mug hit the coaster a little harder than it usually would have done. 'Ellis, I do not want to go on holiday.'

'At least hear me out, Kempston. I mean, look outside. The weather's grotty in Tollinghill at the moment. Can't you just imagine yourself lying on a beach somewhere? Or sitting on a sun-kissed verandah reading a good book, drinking a nice cold lager?'

Hardwick raised one eyebrow.

'Or a Campari and orange,' Ellis added.

'Yes, I can, and I'm sure it would all be very nice but it really is unnecessary. I don't need a holiday.'

Ellis Flint sighed and stood up to fetch the sugar jar. This was going to be an eight-spoon affair.

'Kempston, you're not exactly short of money are you?'

'I am a man of independent means if that's what you're insinuating, Ellis.'

'Right, well why not splash some of that cash on a nice holiday? Come on! Palm trees and warm breezes, foreign culture and architecture. What more could you want?'

Hardwick thought for a few moments. 'Well, I have always wanted to visit the Catacombs of Kom el Shoqafa in northern Egypt.'

'That's the spirit! So is that a yes?' Ellis said.

'I suppose so, yes. I can go down to John Tyler's this afternoon and see what they've got. Listen. Thank you, Ellis. You're a good man,' Hardwick said, before taking another mouthful of his coffee.

'I can go one better,' Ellis said, whipping a pair of tickets from his trouser pocket with a flourish. 'I bought us two tickets yesterday afternoon!'

The realisation struck Hardwick's considerable

brain at the same time as the piece of tomato-stained Artex hit the back of his throat. After much coughing and spluttering, he had regained his composure enough to exclaim just two words.

'*Two? Us?*'

2

The convenient location of London Whitfold airport for many is about its only saving grace. It is, of course, nowhere near London, but in these glorious days of pile-'em-high-sell-'em-cheap budget airlines, anything goes. That is except for the aeroplanes, which rarely go at all and never go on time. Hardwick rued this particular aeronautical idiosyncrasy as he sat silently, sighing inwardly as Ellis Flint popped the sixty-third jelly baby into his mouth.

Whitfold had been the original home of the budget airline in the UK, and it had been at the forefront of a general race to the bottom ever since. A sense of anger and frustration from the majority of travellers, met only by a sense of completely apathy from the staff and ownership, led many local residents to wonder how this small county's own international airport had managed to plunge into the depths of the lowest common denominator of public taste.

Having paid an extortionate amount of money to be dropped off half an hour's walk from the main airport terminal, Hardwick was already less than impressed with the start to his holiday, having had to wake up earlier than usual for it.

Hardwick was used to getting up early, being the sort of chap who tended to rise as soon as the sun did, but he was also a creature of habit. The excited wake-up call from Ellis Flint at four o'clock that morning had done nothing to help matters. Tollinghill was barely half an hour from the airport at most, yet Ellis had insisted they leave plenty of time — 'just in case'. A lack of breakfast and, more importantly, a lack of coffee had meant that Hardwick was feeling rather less tolerant than usual. Now here they were, the sun barely risen, already at the airport three hours ahead of their allotted check-in time.

'Got to make sure we get there nice and early,' Ellis had said. 'Always plenty to do at the airport and at least we know we won't miss our flight.'

Hardwick wouldn't have minded missing the flight.

A holiday was the last thing he wanted, although now he was stuck inside the soulless confines of London Whitfold airport he had begun to long for tropical climes.

'Might go and grab myself a book,' Ellis said through a mouthful of jelly babies. Hardwick was sure he saw at least three little jelly arms attempt a bid for freedom before being crushed by their predator's jaw. 'Quite fancy one of those murder mystery novels, actually.'

'I wouldn't bother, Ellis. The murder mystery novel died out years ago. These days they're all a load of tripe written by bored men with nothing better to do with their lives.'

'I thought you liked murder mysteries,' Ellis said.

'I do. The traditional ones. Only problem is, real-life murders are nothing like the ones in the books. If you read up about real murder cases you'll find they're actually pretty boring.'

'Well it's better than sitting here doing nothing.'

'You're never doing nothing, Ellis.'

Flint made a little noise which sounded like a chipmunk walking into a wall. 'And there's you always saying you shouldn't use a double negative!'

'I didn't. What I meant was, you're always doing

something. Even if you're just sitting quietly, that's what you're doing. Why can people not just sit and mull things over any more? Why must they always be active? Let your brain rest, Ellis. It's probably exhausted after working out the tip for the taxi driver. If you really must do something, you could at least tell me where we're going,' Hardwick said, without having once removed his eyes from his copy of The Times, which was draped across his right leg, which was, in turn, draped over his left leg.

'I told you. Greece.'

'Greece is a big place, Ellis. I hope you've at least narrowed it down a bit,' Hardwick said, trying not to sound too condescending even though his lack of sleep made it even more difficult than usual.

'Well I can't remember the details, can I? It's on the island of Friktos. It looked nice from the pictures. I've got everything written down here, somewhere,' Ellis said, rifling through a manilla folder of papers, receipts and jottings. 'Ah, here we go. The Kollodis Beach Hotel in Kakogoustos. Looks quite nice.'

'Kakogoustos? Very good. Where are we really going?' Hardwick said with a chuckle, a slight hint of nervousness creeping into his voice.

'I just told you,' Ellis replied.

'Ellis, hand me those papers.' Hardwick quickly scanned the text in front of his eyes. 'Oh God. And we have to spend an entire week here?'

'Why? What's wrong with it? It's got a pool and everything,' Ellis said, pointing to the child-filled blob of blue which dominated the page that he had torn out of the brochure a few days previous.

'Oh, I'm sure it has. And a bar which serves a never-ending supply of cold tasteless fizz, a cheap themed "Greek night" and wonderful selection of tattooed bald men.'

'Nonsense. You don't know until you get there. It looks nice in the photos, look,' he said, jabbing his finger at the brochure page again.

'Of course it bloody does! They're not going to advertise it with pictures of men in football shirts smashing glasses over each other's heads, are they? It's Kakogoustos, Ellis. Home of the stiletto heel and the all-night rave. They've made television documentaries about it, for crying out loud. And not even proper ones, either; ones for BBC Three.'

'Our bit might be all right.'

'Our bit might only have a couple of fights each night,' Hardwick said, sarcastically,. 'And maybe we might only tread on a couple of hypodermic needles around the side of the pool.'

'Exactly! See, it isn't so bad after all. Anyway, it's a week away and that's what matters, isn't it?'

Hardwick sighed and returned to the safe refuge of his newspaper. 'If you say so, Ellis.'

3

The flight to the Greek island of Friktos had been just as Hardwick had expected. The first hour and a half was joylessly elongated by the young child sat behind him, who insisted on kicking the back of his chair incessantly, only stopping when its mother presented it with a tablet computer on which it played games and films at full volume for the rest of the flight, its parents seemingly oblivious to the fact that there were other people on the plane. Hardwick, though, had fortunately packed a selection of earplugs and a rather uncharacteristically high level of patience.

Hardwick knew a little about the history of Friktos, but the island rarely made the news these days for any positive reason. Nowadays it was the home of the 18-

30s holiday, where groups of boozed-up Brits would head for a week full of all-inclusive lager, burgers and the resultant puddles of vomit.

The newspapers in England (although not, of course, the type of newspapers Hardwick ever read) were always full of stories about groups of young English adults having been beaten up, stabbed or hospitalised on the island after having had too many drinks and too many fights. It was not exactly Hardwick's idea of a cultural tour of Greece.

Having forced down a slime-filled breeze block (it had been advertised as a cheese panini) and a glass of something almost resembling red wine, Hardwick was looking forward to his first lungful of fresh air as the plane touched down at Kakagoustos International Airport, known locally as Georgios Antonopoulos Airport after the eighteenth-century revolutionary who had attempted to liberate Friktos from the Ottomans in the 1780s — and had succeeded, for a short time.

It was this cultural history of the island which Hardwick was most familiar with, having tried to ignore the Friktos horror stories which had permeated the media in recent years. He took some solace in the fact that he knew there were still some important historical sites on the island, which he'd be certain to visit. Perhaps — just perhaps — he could attempt to make this holiday something verging on the bearable.

As the plane coasted across the tarmac and headed towards the terminal, Hardwick rested his head on the back of his seat and closed his eyes for a few moments. These were likely to be his last few moments of peace.

Ellis, of course, was one of the first people to shoot out of his seat like a jack-in-the-box the second the pilot engaged the parking brake, one hand fumbling around in the overhead compartment as the other concentrated on switching on his mobile phone. An assortment of small objects rained down on the carriage, followed quickly by an assortment of apologies from Ellis, before he finally found his bag and joined the cramped queue headed in the direction of the door.

'Ellis, there's really no need to rush. They have to let everyone off the plane anyway, so why not sit down and wait?' Hardwick said, pulling the well-worn earplugs from the recesses of his ears.

'Don't want to miss a minute of our holiday, do we?' Ellis said, barely noticing Hardwick's raised eyebrow. 'Besides, we'll need to get our cases once we get inside. Be good to get them and go.'

'It's Greece, Ellis. Everything will take ages

anyway,' Hardwick replied, resigned to having to join Ellis in the queue lest he manage to lose him before they'd even got into the airport.

The warm, humid air hit the back of his throat as Hardwick lifted his hand to shield his eyes from the mid-afternoon sun which reflected off the glass facade of the airport terminal. He was thankful that Ellis had convinced him to at least wear a light-coloured suit jacket, if he must wear one at all, and even momentarily considered removing it as the beads of sweat began to form on his forehead.

The sun beat down on them as they walked across the tarmac from the plane to the arrivals entrance, throngs of holidaymakers habitually fumbling around in their bags and pockets for their passports.

On entering the terminal there was a corridor, which meant, of course, that everyone came to an immediate stop and then began to walk at the pace of a dying snail. Hardwick, who was not one for having his pace or activities dictated by others, began to tut in the most English of manners. Ellis was oblivious, humming *Zorba the Greek* to himself as he shuffled his way up the corridor, passport in his clutches.

Having made their way through the arrivals hall and reclaimed their baggage, Hardwick realised it was a day to be thankful for small mercies, as Flint informed him that he had organised a private taxi to the resort as opposed to having opted for the free coach transfer. Being carted around numerous faceless resorts in a tin can full of people he neither knew nor cared for was not Hardwick's idea of fun. Besides which, theirs was bound to be the last drop-off on the list — it always was.

4

The Kollodis Beach Hotel seemed, from the outside at least, to be a fairly pleasant place. Deep-coloured bougainvillaea covered the stone arch-way which led to the main entrance, the white walls of the two-storey building reflecting the warmth of the sun. Hardwick noted the immense din made by the crickets in the dense undergrowth across the road as he hoiked his suitcase up the single step from the pavement to the hotel. If it wasn't for the pulsating dance music he could hear in the background, he could have convinced himself he was on one of the slightly more respectable Greek islands.

From here he could see the pool, and he quickly realised that he had been quite right in his assumptions about the place. Groups of people toasted themselves under the sun as the dance music pounded across the complex, the only saving grace seeming to be that, thanks to it being term-time, there seemed to be no young children around.

Although he'd had very little sleep and he didn't really want to be here, Hardwick looked around and tried to focus on the positives. The flowers were very nice, if a little wilted in the heat. The crickets were clearly having a lovely time, too, so it can't have been that bad.

There was a mountain in the distance which certainly improved the view, and he focused on this as he reminded himself that he'd make sure he got to see some of the few remaining historical sites on Friktos before the week was out. A week. Just a week, then he'd be back home in the Old Rectory. Smiling for the first time that day, he followed Ellis into the entrance to the hotel, watching him struggle to pull his suitcase inside as Ellis's digital watch beeped to indicate that it was three o'clock in the afternoon.

'What on earth have you got in there?' Hardwick asked him when they got into the reception area.

'All sorts. Always better to bring too much than have to go without, eh? And there's nothing worse than having stuff rattle around in your suitcase, so much safer to bring as much as you can.'

The woman on the reception desk seemed to be less than enthusiastic about her job, despite it being air-conditioned. The air conditioning, though, was negated by the amount of hot air coming from the woman who was stood talking to — or, rather, at — the receptionist at that moment.

'We specifically asked for a sea view!' the woman barked, banging her fist on the reception desk.

'Madam, we do not offer a sea view. We have instead given you a pool view,' the receptionist offered in her very best English.

'Well I don't bloody well want a pool view, do I? Why on earth would I want to sit and watch a load of people splashing about in a pool?'

Despite the complaining woman being somewhere around her late twenties, she seemed to carry an air of pretension which even Hardwick found impressive.

'Madam, we are not near the sea. It is not possible to have a sea view from here. I'm sorry, but this is all we have,' said the receptionist, trying her very best to look apologetic whilst quite clearly not giving a toss. After a few more huffs and puffs, the woman, who Hardwick had overheard checking in as Jennifer Alexander, went to join her embarrassed partner and friends who had been waiting sheepishly with their suitcases in the corner of the reception area, trying desperately to look as if they were engrossed in the holiday company's ring-bound guide to the local area.

Hardwick and Flint stepped forward. 'Your reservation paper, please?' the receptionist said, for the umpteenth time that day, jabbing her computer keyboard as she tapped their names into the system. 'OK, I have here just one room, yes?'

'Yes, please. A twin room.' Flint replied, before turning to Hardwick. 'It was much cheaper that way. Two rooms would've cost a bomb.'

'Ah. You see, we have here a double room,' the receptionist said, pointing at her computer.

'Oh. Right. Well, is it possible to separate the bed at all?' Ellis asked, sensing that Hardwick was already starting to bubble over the edge of his comfort zone. 'Or is there perhaps a sofa in the apartment? We're just friends, you see. We don't really want to be sharing a bed.'

'Please, sir,' the receptionist said. 'We are very open-minded in Greece. We practically invented it.'

'Invented what?' Ellis began to ask, but the woman had already lifted his bulging suitcase with one hand

and began to lug it down the pathway towards their apartment.

* * *

The apartment was very spacious and very Greek. The cold terracotta-tiled floor was pure bliss compared to the heat outside, and Ellis quickly kicked off his shoes and began to make steamy footprints on the tiles as he thudded around the apartment inspecting every inch of it.

'Look, Kempston! They've got a kettle!' he said, with the excitement of a school boy.

'You've got a kettle at home, Ellis. It's not exactly the cutting edge of technology.'

'No, but you don't expect to see one when you're on holiday, do you? I told you we'd like this place. It's the little things, isn't it? Makes all the difference,' he said, before gawping in awe at the fifteen-year-old television.

'Ellis, it's Greece, not Mordor. They do make tea and coffee here as well, you know. I bet it's probably better coffee than you make, too,' Hardwick said, sitting down on the sofa.

'To be fair, they are known for their coffee. I

suppose that's why it's called Greek coffee,' Ellis said philosophically. 'Probably not as sweet as I make it, though.'

'Less tomatoey too, I should imagine,' Hardwick murmured, plunging his hands into the cushions on the sofa. 'This sofa's pretty comfortable, actually. Shouldn't hurt your bad back at all,' he added, before getting up, grabbing his bag and marching towards the bedroom before Ellis could say another word.

5

Hardwick had convinced Ellis that it would be far better to go out to dinner early (thereby preceding the hordes of tourists) before heading back to the pool bar for a couple of nightcaps. After all, they had been up ridiculously early that morning and could then make the most of the following days. Ellis, fortunately, agreed.

They'd headed into town around six-thirty that evening and were back at the hotel bar by just gone eight. The restaurant had been a fairly pleasant affair: a traditional Greek taverna which Hardwick had found by heading off the beaten track, feeling very pleased with himself as they enjoyed a carafe of wine and calamari followed by a Greek salad. He'd go for the moussaka one evening when they'd come out to eat later, when it would be a little less warm and humid.

The walk back from the restaurant to the apartment complex took them down a winding hillside road and onto the main strip of Kakagoustos, although thankfully only for a couple of minutes before they veered off to the north in the direction of their apartment complex and away from the centre of the town. Even now, at barely eight o'clock in the evening, they could hear the music thump-thumping from the town, the laser lights beginning to cast their symbols and messages into the night sky and onto the face of the mountain behind the town.

At this time of night, the setting of the apartment complex was spectacular. The bamboo bar sat just yards away from the azure blue pool, which in the evenings was lit up by a collection of underwater lights. Visually, it was beautiful. The only assault on Hardwick's senses came from the dance music, which continued to pulse, and the undiscerning and obnoxious noise coming from some of the other guests.

The main culprits seemed to be a group of three men in their early twenties who were sat at the opposite side of the circular bar, trying keenly and loudly to impress their alpha male credentials on two girls who seemed to be a couple of years younger than them. One of the pack appeared to have snared his prey, his arm draped casually around one of the girls' necks, his other hand placed firmly on the inside of her thigh.

Hardwick also noticed the group of four who had been in front of him and Ellis in the reception queue earlier that day, who were now sat at one of the tables surrounding the bar. The sea-view woman seemed to be a little more placated after a few drinks, but still seemed somewhat aloof in her body language, opting for crossed arms and a stern look on her face. Hardwick, who had by now had half a carafe of wine and a couple of Camparis and orange, wondered innocently how people could be so miserable when they were away for the week.

Sea-view woman's partner had also gone for the arm-around-the-shoulder move, with their friends — another couple — sat opposite, laughing and joking over an enormous fishbowl full of some sort of suspicious-looking cocktail.

The barman seemed to be in full spirits, seemingly enjoying his role of alcohol supplier and master of ceremonies in between the quiet moments when he'd just sit and play on his mobile phone.

'He's going to drop one of those in a minute,' Ellis

Flint remarked, pointing at the barman, who was juggling an array of cocktail shakers and glasses as the easily-impressed holidaymakers looked on.

'Yes, well he'll get a clip round the ear if he tries doing that with my Campari,' Hardwick replied.

Ellis raised his eyebrow in mock concern. 'You know, I think that's the first violent remark I've ever heard you make.'

Hardwick seemed somewhat regretful and apologetic, and started tugging at his jacket. 'Yes, well I think the heat is just getting to me.'

'I'm not bloody surprised! You're wearing a suit jacket in this heat! Eight o'clock in the evening and it's still thirty-odd degrees. I think you can afford to dress a little more casually in this weather,' said Ellis Flint, who was sweating buckets in his t-shirt and shorts.

'I am dressed casually, Ellis. I'm wearing chinos.'

'Chinos aren't casual! Especially when you're wearing a suit jacket with them.'

'It's light-coloured.'

'And still far too warm for this weather. Come on, get it off!' Ellis shouted, having got up from his stool and started tugging at the back of the jacket. Hardwick's protestations soon drew the attention of the group sat opposite.

'Wahey! Can't you boys wait 'til you get back to your room for that?'

'Got yourself an animal there, mate!' another one added, laughing.

It had all got a little too much for Hardwick. 'Ellis, will you *get off of my bloody jacket?*' The rare outburst took Ellis by surprise, and he did as he was told. Very quickly. Acquiescing to his greater common sense, though, Hardwick removed his jacket and hung it over the back of his stool.

'Better?'

'Just trying to help,' Flint replied.

'There's no need to be blunt, Ellis.'

'I'm not.'

Before Hardwick could even consider biting his tongue, one of the men from the table of four appeared at his other side, having come up to the bar to order some more drinks.

'I was wondering when you were going to take that jacket off. Must be mad wearing that in this weather,' the man said.

'Oh, for... Why is everyone so concerned about my bloody jacket?' Hardwick asked incredulously.

'Just saying, like. Didn't mean to cause offence.'

The man shrunk into himself visibly, at which Hard-wick let out a sigh.

'I'm sorry. I'm just a bit ratty. I'm not really one for holidays, if I'm honest.'

'Few drinks inside you, you'll be fine,' the man said, pointing at Hardwick's glass. 'Can I get you one?'

'Very kind, thank you,' Hardwick replied. 'A Campari and orange, if you don't mind.'

6

The man ordered the drinks from the barman, who had momentarily stopped throwing glass objects around. As the drinks were being poured, the sea-view woman came to join the man at the bar.

'Think we're going to sit up here. Those wicker chairs really dig into the back of my legs,' she said, having carted the other two in their group up to the bar with her. Her tight red dress seemed almost to have been tailored for her body; a body which Ellis Flint had duly noted and considered his approval of. It struck Hardwick that perhaps the old maxim was true that you either had looks or personality, but rarely both.

'I'm James, by the way,' the man who'd ordered the

drinks said, offering his hand to Hardwick and Flint, who both introduced themselves in return. The man went on to introduce his red-dressed sea-loving girl-friend, Jennifer (who insisted that she was his *"fiancée, actually"*), and their friends, Darryl and Alicia, who were also a couple and were friends of James and Jennifer.

James and Jennifer appeared to be in their late twenties, as did Alicia, although Darryl was slightly older — late thirties, Hardwick would've guessed. It was Darryl who did most of the talking, although he never said anything of any real note, while Jennifer seemed to dominate the group silently and with the odd well-placed comment which could turn the whole conversation on its head. The odd dynamic was not lost on Hardwick.

It wasn't long before the conversation was flowing, as were the drinks, and the group of the three loud boys and two girls were also at the bar, throwing back shots of a clear liquid, the pungently sweet smell of aniseed making Hardwick feel slightly ill. He was, however, quite happy to accept their continual offers of more Campari and orange, never one to turn down the offer of a free drink.

Hardwick and James continued to chat for the next half an hour, with Ellis Flint quite happily and merrily helping the younger lads demolish another bottle of ouzo. James had already told Hardwick that he was a civil servant, working in a local planning department dealing with industrial and commercial planning. Even to Hardwick this was something of a less-than-interesting subject, but the way James spoke made even the most tedious of subjects sound interesting and engaging. The pair had discovered mutual loves of travel, good books and the arts.

James had told Hardwick of the travels he'd been on in his gap year (which had actually been two years), backpacking around Australia, travelling across Vietnam and China and having seen a fair bit of Eastern Europe.

'It's the Balkan cities which are the most incredible these days,' he said. 'You go to Belgrade or Sarajevo now and you'd be amazed. You'd think you were in London or New York. Although you've got to do those sorts of countries in a certain order. Still some animosity between them in places. You travelled around much?'

'Quite a lot as a child,' Hardwick told him. 'My parents were environmental scientists, in the early days. We moved around all over the place. Patagonia, Siberia, India, the Far East.'

'Wow. You must have seen a lot then,' James said.

'Yes. Too much,' Hardwick replied, not going into any detail.

'It's rare I ever get to speak to anyone about stuff like this,' he said. 'I'm usually stuck around the house sorting things out for Jennifer and don't get to go out all that much.'

'Don't your friends share the same interests?' Hardwick asked, gesturing towards the remaining three in his group.

James made a noise that sounded like a car doing an emergency stop on gravel. 'They're Jennifer's friends.'

'You don't get on?'

'No, not especially. I mean, Alicia's all right sometimes and generally pretty harmless, but Darryl and I... well, we don't see eye to eye.' James took a slurp of his drink. Hardwick could see James's teeth grinding as he spoke about his dislike of Darryl. 'He's arrogant, selfish and rude. Not my sort of bloke at all.'

'So why are you on holiday with them, may I ask?'

James took a deep breath and exhaled as he spoke. 'Jennifer and Alicia are best friends. Have been since junior school. To be honest, she's about the only real friend she's got left.'

'I see. Does it not bother you having to come on holiday with them?'

'Nah. Like I said, I don't mind Alicia. As long as I'm able to avoid Darryl or pretend he's not there... well, a holiday's a holiday ain't it?'

Hardwick chuckled quietly to himself. 'Yes. Yes, I suppose it is.'

The forceful slap on the back told Hardwick that Ellis Flint had perhaps demolished a little too much of the ouzo.

'Kempston, you beast! How's it hanging?' he said, as he hung off Hardwick's neck with one arm and prodded him in the face with his free hand.

'Just fine, Ellis, thank you.'

'You know, those lads are really something. You wouldn't believe the sorts they've pulled this week!'

'Yes, lovely. Would you like a pint of water?'

'No, I want a b-beer. Something long and cold so I can watch these smooth operators in action!' Ellis slurred as he pointed over to the table James had vacated earlier. Darryl was nowhere to be seen, but the three lads Ellis had been drinking with were now swarming around Jennifer and Alicia like a pack of dogs.

'Isn't that your girlfriend?' Hardwick asked James, who sipped his drink with greater alacrity than usual, his face reddening by the second.

'Yes. Loving the attention, I'm sure,' he replied, a little too calmly.

'Don't you want to... well, stop it?' Hardwick said as he watched one of the lads' hands crawl up Jennifer's leg like a possessed tarantula.

Before James could reply, Jennifer had pushed the lad (who Ellis told Hardwick was called Nick) away and slapped him across the side of his face. The bamboo-framed chairs scraping on tiles sounded like an orchestra tuning up as the other two predators realised their prey was not playing ball this time.

7

The lads soon skulked off back in the direction of the table they'd previously been sitting at and said very little. Alicia seemed to be trying to placate Jennifer and inject a bit of humour in order to defuse the situation, but Jennifer instead opted to shoot daggers at the lads, who were sat like a pack of scolded puppies with their tails between their legs.

'Looks like she's told them what's what,' Ellis said, taking another long slurp of his pint.

'Yeah, once he had his hand up her dress,' James replied. 'Bloody lucky, too. Blokes like that don't deserve any respect. If they can't respect women, they deserve everything that's coming to them.'

It was then that James spotted Darryl sauntering

back across the complex from the direction of the toilet block on the other side of the pool, seemingly oblivious to what had just happened.

'What the bloody hell do you think you're doing?' James barked at Darryl as he got back to the table, an unexpected air of confidence and bravado having come over him.

'Er, having a slash. That all right with you?'

'No! Not when you bugger off and leave these two on their own to be set upon by bloody Casanova and Co. over there!' James shouted back, jabbing his finger in the direction of Nick, Paul and Ryan. '

'Oh, right, OK,' Darryl replied,' taking a step towards James so that their faces were inches apart and their chests were almost touching. I'll just sit here and piss myself then, shall I, because you're not man enough to stand up for your own bird?'

The stockier of the three lads, known as Paul, had got up and put his arm between James and Darryl and offered his own form of apology. 'Listen, we didn't mean anything by it, all right? It's just Nick and the way he is. No offence meant, yeah? Let's just forget about it and have a drink.'

'"Just the way he is"?' Jennifer said in a mocking tone of voice as she rose from her chair to confront

Paul. 'Well if you know what he's like, then why the hell did you even let him bother in the first place? I'll tell you why,' she said, before he could even answer the question. 'It's because you're a pathetic, weak little fat man. You wouldn't stand a chance with me if you were the last bloke on Earth, now piss off back to your sad little friends.'

Paul said nothing, but nodded sagely before turning and heading back to Ryan and Nick at the other table.

Darryl, meanwhile, had stood at the bar and taken his mobile phone out of his pocket in a manly look-how-much-I-don't-care kind of way. Hardwick was no expert on modern technology — far from it — but even he recognised it straight away as a fairly new iPhone, with the bright, rich colours of the screen showing off the beauty of the picture of a hyacinth which Darryl had set as his phone's background wallpaper.

The situation seemed to have calmed for a moment, with the three lads keeping much quieter and more subdued than they had been up until that point, now speaking quietly to Emma and Hayley on the table next to them. Jennifer was sat back in her chair, saying nothing but instead opting to reapply her makeup, which she was inspecting in her compact mirror.

By this point, the long-haired glass-juggling Albanian barman, who had earlier introduced himself as Arjun before proceeding to do very little other than lean back on his stool against the glass-washer and put his feet up on the bar while playing games on his own mobile phone, had finally decided to pipe up.

'Eh, peace, people,' he said in one of his heavily accented mock-English catchphrases which he'd perfected to impress the type of holidaymakers who found that sort of thing funny. 'Happy times. Happy happy. Let's all get pissed, eh?'

8

By nine-thirty, Ellis Flint was beginning to seem rather sober compared with Hardwick, who'd dealt with the stresses of the evening by taking it out on another bottle of Campari. Hardwick was never one to seem outwardly inebriated, but even he recognised that the control he had over his vast brain was beginning to slip. The worrying thing was that he didn't mind one bit.

He was never really one to suffer from hangovers. This was something which made Ellis Flint insanely jealous, as two swigs of mouthwash the previous evening would have his head pounding the next morning. For Hardwick, though, a six-o'clock rise and a brisk walk would have him set up perfectly for the day. Safe in that knowledge, he took another sip of his drink and smiled.

The hotel's owner, a fat man with a thick moustache and sweat patches on his shirt, had been sat on one stool for the best part of half an hour, ensuring that those holidaymakers with a sense of smell had gravitated to the exact polar opposite of the circular bar. He'd taken to engaging the guests in conversation, but their noses were thankful where their ears were not, as he seemed to have the habit of shouting his words to whomever he was speaking, from wherever he was sat. Distance was no object for this man's talent for projecting his voice, and he seemed to revel in having conversations with people who were as far away as possible.

Nick, Paul and Ryan had now merged tables with the two younger girls, Hayley and Emma. While Ryan was busy playing tonsil tennis with Emma and Nick was having a heated squabble with Hayley, Paul sat back and flicked through the social networking app on his smartphone, trying his level best to seem oblivious to the romantic episodes carrying on around him.

From what Hardwick could overhear (and he was an experienced and practised overhearer) Hayley had been having some sort of holiday fling with Nick, and wasn't best pleased at seeing that he'd tried his luck with Jennifer earlier that evening. Nick's point of view had been that his relationship with Hayley was hardly a serious one, and that she shouldn't get het up about it. Hayley disagreed and ensured that Nick had a matching palm-print on his other cheek.

By nine forty-five Nick and Hayley's disagreement seemed to have died down, as they latched onto each other like a pair of Chinese sucker fish, the events of the evening seemingly forgotten. Unfortunately, the wind had started to increase slightly, much to the revulsion of the guests who were seated downwind of Stavros, the hotel's owner. Fortunately for them, this was also the time that he had bellowed to everyone that he needed to disappear off to his office to do some work on his accounts.

The atmosphere continued to be somewhat strained, although Nick, Paul and Ryan were doing their level best to keep spirits high, having cajoled Ellis, Hayley and Emma into doing the *Macarena* at the side of the pool. Hardwick, who wasn't hungry and didn't like burgers, instead opted to read the burger menu for the fortieth time that evening.

James, Jennifer, Darryl and Alicia were starting to feel the effects of the sun, drinks and long day, and the tension in their group was still palpable although the conversation had since turned to more pleasant subjects.

'I'm probably going to go up to bed, make the most of tomorrow. I'm not feeling great,' Alicia said, rubbing her eyes and forehead.

'It's the sun. You're probably just tired,' Jennifer said authoritatively.

'Yeah, probably. Just need to get my head down, I think. What time are we meeting for breakfast?'

'Nine o'clock, we said earlier,' Darryl replied. 'Although it'll be a miracle if any of us are up by then. Think I'm going to have a bit of a head on me anyway. I'll take her back,' he said to the others. 'Make sure she's all right.'

'I am still here, you know,' Alicia replied. 'I'll be fine. I'm just not feeling great.'

'Well you don't look fine, and I just want to sit with you for a bit and make sure you're not going to be ill. Come on,' he said, as he helped escort her across the poolside area towards their apartment.

James bought another round of drinks for himself, Jennifer and Darryl, and placed the latter two's on the table before standing at the bar and chatting to Hardwick, who was the only other holidaymaker who wasn't dancing like a lunatic at the side of the pool.

'Bit embarrassing, isn't it?' James said.

'Not for us it isn't,' Hardwick said with a wry smile. 'Your friends gone to bed, have they?'

'Alicia has. I think Darryl's coming back. Just wants to make sure she gets off to sleep. She's not feeling too good, apparently.'

'Oh dear. Nothing serious, I hope?' Hardwick asked.

'Oh, no. Just tiredness. Too much sun and alcohol, I reckon.'

'Well, I hope she feels better soon.'

James was about to reply when his girlfriend tugged at his elbow like a petulant child.

'James, am I going to be sat here on my own all night?'

'No, sweetheart, I'm just talking to Kempston. Darryl'll be back in a minute anyway. I won't be long.'

The look on Jennifer's face said it all as she flounced off back to her table.

'Maybe you should get back to her. She doesn't seem too happy,' Hardwick sagely pointed out.

'Well she's going to have to learn to deal with it, isn't she?' James replied, with the air of a man who was finally starting to stand up to his tormentor. 'Anyway, it's a point of principle. I'm getting fed up with just having to jump every time she clicks her fingers. Maybe it's the drink talking, but I'm standing my ground. I want to talk to you, and that's that.'

'Very well,' Hardwick said. 'Another drink, then?'

9

Barely twenty-five minutes later, at around ten-thirty, Jennifer had decided enough was enough, polished off her drink and marched off back towards their apartment, having delivered James a parting shot of: 'Well, I'm not just going to sit here on my own like some sort of loser.'

Hardwick had already formed his own thoughts on Jennifer, as he so often and so quickly did with people, but nonetheless felt it necessary to probe a little further into their relationship now that James had been suitably lubricated with drink.

'Does she always speak to you like that?' he asked.

'Yep. And worse. She's used to getting her own way. An only child. Her parents spoilt her rotten.

They were told they'd never be able to have children, so when she came along they treated her like she was some sort of goddess. Problem is, she still thinks she is one. She's got no friends left, other than Alicia, and that's only because she's a mouse, like me. We don't stand up for ourselves and she knows it, so she ends up walking all over us.'

'I presume you're happy with her, though?' Hardwick asked.

'I guess so. I don't really know. Truth be told, we've been together since high school so I guess I just don't know any different. Things happen gradually, don't they? It's only when you look back and see the person you used to be and the person you are now that you realise what massive changes have happened without you even noticing. It's the same with Alicia — she's known her since they were kids, but Alicia's always been quiet.'

'Does Darryl not get upset with her treating Alicia badly?'

'I dunno. I try not to speak to him, so I can't say. But he's just as bad — pig-headed and arrogant, so he probably doesn't see that there's anything wrong with her.'

'Sounds like Darryl and Jennifer should be the

couple to me,' Hardwick said, before stopping, real-ising what he'd just said.

'Don't worry about it,' James said, sensing Hard-wick's discomfort. 'No offence taken. It's a no-go, though. I think the world would end if those two ever got together. I think they'd need to live in a padded house.'

'There's an age difference between them, isn't there?' Hardwick asked.

'Yeah, about ten years or so. Darryl's always had younger girlfriends, though, from what I've heard. Sort of bloke who's never ready to grow up and settle down. Bit of a drifter, a waster.'

'What does he do for work?'

'Whatever he needs to to get enough money. He's not exactly a career bloke. He's worked in pubs, done labouring, bit of delivery driving. Means to an end for him, I suppose. Alicia's the career-driven one. She's always worked in banking. Not city-level stuff, like — just local branch stuff.'

A few minutes later the conversation had started to die down and the events of the evening were clearly playing on James's mind.

'Listen,' he said. 'I'd better go and check on her. Make sure she's all right.' Spotting Hardwick's raised eyebrow, he added: 'I'll come back in a bit. Just want to try and make sure she's not going to be pissed off forever. I've got to spend another week cooped up here with her, after all.'

James took a sip of his beer, leaving half a pint sat on the bar as a gesture of his impending return, and walked back towards the apartment.

Left only with Arjun, the Albanian barman and the rejects from *Come Dancing*, Hardwick finally decided to strike up conversation with the semi-reclined Arjun.

'Do you live here all year round, then?'

'No,' Arjun replied. 'I go back to Albania in winter. I work on building sites. My father has business there. There are a lot of new houses being built in Albania. Also a lot of hotels in tourist areas.'

'Oh right. And do they pay you well here?'

'Not too bad. Stavros gives me apartment for summer and I take percentage from drinks here. In my town in Albania is no building in summer. Is too hot, and everyone is being involved in tourism.'

'What town's that?' Hardwick asked curiously, being the well-traveled man that he was.

'Sarandë, in the south. Since the civil war we have had many tourists now, enjoying the weather and culture. Is also a tourist area, but money is more here.'

'I see. You enjoy it, then?'

'Is OK. Sometimes is fun, sometimes is not so much,' Arjun said, gesticulating towards the apartment block.

'Ah, right. The guests,' Hardwick deduced.

'No!' Arjun said forcefully, as if Hardwick had said something terribly wrong. 'The guests are fantastic. Problem is owner.' Hardwick's raised eyebrow signalled that Arjun should continue. 'This place is earning no money for years, since recession. In Greece now is very hard to earn money. I am not running business, so is no problem for me. For Stavros, though, is very stressful. Sometimes this makes him angry.'

'Yes, well, I'm sure it's much the same for business owners across the world at the moment,' Hardwick said, trying to defuse Arjun's macabre tone.

'No. Is different,' was his only reply as he leant back, resigned, and took out his smartphone.

'Looks like I'm in the dog house,' James said nervously as he arrived back at Hardwick's side.

'She still angry?' Hardwick asked.

'Bloody well seems like it. I was stood there knocking on the door but she wouldn't let me in.'

'Did she say anything?'

'Oh, God yeah. Plenty of things. None which I'm going to repeat in more pleasant company, though. Looks like I'm sleeping on a sun lounger tonight.'

'Think yourself lucky you're in Friktos, then,' Hardwick said without a hint of irony. 'Lovely weather for it.'

'Yeah, well it's definitely going to be pretty bloody icy cold in that bedroom tonight, that's for sure.'

'Join me for another drink, then?'

'Just the one?' James replied with a smile.

10

James and Hardwick's conversation continued, both having become fairly well acquainted with each other as the night had gone on. Ellis had carried on drinking with Nick, Paul and Ryan and had learnt a whole host of new dance moves which he was keen on showing to Hardwick at every given opportunity. After a while, Hardwick stopped giving him opportunities.

By quarter past eleven, Nick had also decided he'd had enough of the evening and declared that he, too, was off to bed, whether the others liked it or not. Paul and Ryan, seemingly oblivious to the company of Hayley and Emma, called out: 'Off to try and get a bit of that Jennifer bird are you?' before collapsing into fits of laughter.

Nick, though, wasn't laughing. Whether tired or just plain inebriated, his words were strangely calm and confident. 'Don't worry, lads,' he said, before glancing over at James. 'I'll get my bit.'

The laughter quickly died down and became a hushed mumbling, with Hardwick having to place his hand on James's forearm to stop him going after Nick. Ellis sat beside Paul and Ryan, looking slightly embarrassed and very drunk. No words were said between James and Hardwick, but the sentiment was clear.

'Everyone's had a couple of drinks. They're young and they're trying to make themselves seem bigger than they are,' Hardwick said, this being as philosophical as he could get after a few drinks and a day of sun.

'Yeah, well. The first time's funny, the second time's a bit of a pain. After it's been happening all night it kind of grates, y'know?'

Hardwick simply nodded.

'I mean, it's not as if she's out on her own or with a group of girls, is it? She's on holiday with me, so they're clearly just doing it to try and wind me up. Makes it worse in a way — they're not even doing it because they're particularly interested in her.'

* * *

Midnight came, and Hayley and Emma took that as their cue to leave, having finished sipping their bright blue cocktails and said goodnight to Ellis, Ryan and Paul, who were starting to look a little worse for wear. Ellis decided he was going to order one more drink, offering Hardwick and James another round.

'Don't you think you've had a few too many already, Ellis?' Hardwick asked him.

'We all have,' were the words that Ellis managed to squeeze out of his lips, which were now blubbering about like a pair of beached whales. 'We're on holiday, Kempston. You've got to looshen up a bit and have shome fun. Wassa problem?'

'No problem here, Ellis. Just bear in mind that I'll be waking you up bright and early tomorrow. Probably best if your headache isn't too extreme,' Hardwick said, his words being perfectly enunciated as always, despite his own brain swimming in Campari.

'It's fine. One more. Then bed.'

'Very well, Ellis. Anyway, I'm sure you can keep up with your newfound friends. Despite the age difference.'

'Age difference?' Ellis asked, so astounded by Hardwick's comment that he almost lost his balance as he jerked his upper body backwards. Balance, though, was not Ellis's greatest strength right now.

'Well, come on. Look at you. And at them. You could be their father.'

'Doubt it. I've never been to Middlesbrough.'

'No, that's not... I mean you're about twenty-five years older than they are.'

'So?' Ellis replied.

Hardwick saw no point in replying. The state Ellis was in right now, anything would have seemed like a good idea to him.

So it was, then, that another round was bought. Hardwick tried to mentally calculate how many drinks each of them had had that night, but he couldn't even work out how many he'd had himself. Good job it was cheap, he thought, or there'd be some aching wallets tomorrow morning as well as heads.

Having finished their final round of drinks, Ellis, Paul and Ryan headed back to their apartments, the latter two propping Ellis up with an arm round each of their shoulders.

'We'll get him back to bed, Kempston. Think he's had a bit too much!' Ryan called, Ellis's flip-flopped feet skidding across the tiles as Paul and Ryan took his weight.

'See you in the morning, Ellis,' he replied. 'Bright and early.'

With only Hardwick, James and the barman, Arjun, still at the bar, Arjun began to make it pretty clear that he was keen to get to bed.

'Is busy here, you know. Not just in evening, but during day as well. Every morning I am up six o'clock to clean pool.'

'Really? How remarkable,' Hardwick replied, never keen on people trying to infer meanings when they could just perfectly well come out and say them.

'Also then to prepare breakfast, clean the sun beds and sweep the pool area.'

'Mmmm, you do a good job.'

'Yes. Is long hours, and hard work. Very tired in the summer. Maybe four hours to sleep in night. I have to clean and tidy bar after evenings as well.'

'Well it looks very nice for it. A good job.'

By twelve-thirty, James had been unable to suppress his titters and had openly suggested that they should call it a night. Hardwick agreed, bade Arjun goodnight and escorted the somewhat-tipsy James across to his sun lounger for the night before heading back to his apartment. Stumbling around in the pitch black, he silently cursed the hotel's owner for not lighting up the pathway towards the apartments. None of the apartments or doors were particularly discernible, but fortunately for him, Ellis had left the porch light on and the number '3' was plenty visible. Less than five minutes later, he was sound asleep.

11

Hardwick always woke up when the sun rose. Today, it was six o'clock in the morning and his vast mind was awake and buzzing with the thought of another day.

He was always thankful to have woken up and experienced another day. After some of the things he'd seen, it always stunned him to realise that no-one ever knew when their last day on earth would be. It could be any of us at any time and he had seen his fair share of untimely deaths. For that reason more than any, he always embraced every new day.

The crickets were already buzzing away outside the window, and Hardwick got dressed and headed into the living area of the apartment. Ellis was still unconscious on the sofa, sleeping off the excesses of the previous night. Even the boiling of the kettle didn't wake him as Hardwick made his customary mug of coffee and sat on the verandah to drink it.

The morning sun was simply stunning. Already warm and soothing without the intense searing hit which would come later in the day. A Mediterranean early morning was like a British summer's afternoon. Just right.

The early morning had always been his favourite time of day. It was the start, the freshest part of the day, unspoilt by the events which were inevitably to come. It brought hope and potential. More than anything, it was quiet.

It's a fact — there are too many people on this earth. That's why Hardwick liked the early morning, when the vast majority of them were still tucked up in their beds, not yet taking part in the unfolding of the day. Leaving it all for him.

Having finished his coffee and put on his shoes, Hardwick left the apartment and headed in the direction of the town. He noticed that the door to the end apartment, two doors down, was slightly ajar. More early risers, Hardwick mused to himself. More people who liked to take advantage of the glorious morning sun.

The pavement ran alongside the road into the centre of Kakagoustos, although for the first hundred yards or so it was nothing but a dirt track. The Kollidis Beach Hotel (which wasn't strictly a hotel) was right on the edge of the town. Be thankful for small mercies, Hardwick told himself.

As he reached the edge of the shops and restaurants, men with moustaches and beer bellies were hauling piles of newspapers off of low-loaders and dumping them outside the shops, which would not be open for some hours yet.

Another similar low-loader was carrying hundreds of huge bottles of water, ready to be consumed by the hordes of tourists who'd been poisoning themselves by throwing gallons of ouzo down their necks every night but somehow deemed themselves incapable of digesting Greek water without turning into Frankenstein's monster. 'The mineral content's higher than we're used to,' they'd say. Well hell, why not get yourself used to a higher mineral content, then? Or just stick to the chlorine-packed copper-poisoned rubbish which pours out of the taps in your home back in England. Proper English water, they call it. The same people who refused to eat 'that foreign muck', and instead decided to opt to spend the week guzzling burgers and chips.

No worries — another couple of hundred yards and the fresh morning air would make him a little less grumpy. That is assuming he could ignore the sight and stench of the discarded burger cartons and beer bottles which were scattered around the centre of the town. Already the morning sun had begun to warm them up, speeding up the process of decomposition and releasing the foul, sweet and sickly stench which emanates from all bins in hot countries. And Kakagoustos that morning was a bin.

The area around the bars and nightclubs was like a ghost town. At least two nightclubs were just locking their doors after another evening's business, their customers having long fallen into their drunken stupor back at their own hotel rooms. The centre of town was eerily silent. Whilst most others around the world were just gearing up for the day, at this time of the morning Kakagoustos was asleep and probably wouldn't wake up until the day was already in its closing stages. So not only did these people not want the foreign food or the foreign water, but they didn't even want the foreign weather.

* * *

By seven o'clock, Hardwick was back at the poolside, still the only holidaymaker who seemed to be up and awake, apart from James, who was still on his sun lounger, looking slightly less than comfortable but perfectly happy all the same. He'd clearly been woken up by the searing morning sun, as he seemed to have got up and fetched a parasol, which he'd erected to create some semblance of shade as he slept.

Arjun, the barman, had already hosed down the tiles around the pool and was busy fishing leaves and small creatures out of the swimming pool. He accidentally dripped his fishing net over James, who woke with a start. James very quickly decided the best course of action would be a large glass of water and some aspirin, which Arjun scuttled off to fetch for him as James rubbed his head and cracked out the knots in his back from the night spent on the sun lounger.

'Good night's sleep?' Hardwick asked with a smirk.

'Had better. Still, better to let Jennifer calm down for a bit. Wouldn't have done me much good to go back there last night.'

'Well, hopefully she'll have calmed down and seen sense by the time she gets up,' Hardwick offered.

'Probably. She's pretty irritating like that. Sure, she can hold a grudge, but she's also got this uncanny way of being able to just forget about something if it suits her. Wouldn't surprise me one bit if she seemed absolutely fine. Women, eh?'

Hardwick, who tried to have very little to do with romantic relationships of any kind, just smiled.

12

Ellis Flint had woken up with a hangover that raged like Dante's Inferno. He hadn't yet dared to open his eyes but he knew that he must. He always had weird thoughts after he'd been drinking. What *would* happen if he just got up and got on with his day but never once opened his eyes? Would he feel any better? Hell, it was bad enough now when his eyes were closed. He dreaded opening them. He knew he had to. Couldn't go around the whole day with his eyes shut. Just the one for now, then, he decided, and steered his one eye towards the clock on the side table.

Just gone half seven. That was a good sign. If he was feeling pretty rough now, it was good that it was early. A sign that he'd probably feel all right by lunchtime. It was when you woke up at ten or eleven feeling like this that it was going to be a painful one.

Not knowing whether he needed a hair of the dog (the thought made him feel physically sick) or simply a nice greasy bacon butty, he convinced himself he needed to get up. He pulled one leg over onto the floor and eased himself up onto his elbow. His neck and back ached like hell from sleeping on the sofa all night. With the amount he'd had to drink, he probably hadn't moved all night. He gently rolled his neck and arched his back, being extra careful to make sure his spine hadn't actually set in place overnight.

His head was thick with the hangover, and his mouth tasted like a badger's backside. He could almost feel the fur. The thought made him feel physically ill, but strangely much better than the thought of another drink.

He eased himself up further until he was sat up, his back arched over, the rolls of fat from his beer-bloated belly rested on his lap. Breakfast. That'd sort it. Sure, it was Greece, but even here they must be able to rustle up a nice warm bacon butty, dripping with fat. And coffee. Lots of coffee. His stomach rumbled at the thought, and Ellis translated that as a wholehearted agreement and stumbled to his feet before heading to the bathroom.

He splashed some cold water on his face, changed his underwear and put on a pair of shorts and a t-shirt before fumbling around for a few minutes trying to unlock the door to get out of the apartment.

The sun hit him full in the face like a punch from Mohammed Ali. He visibly took a step back, his cheeks puffed out as he felt the assault on his entire body, reaching desperately for his sunglasses. They said sun was good for the metabolism. Ellis hoped it'd speed his up pretty quickly and get rid of the alcohol which was making him feel like a dead man walking.

He stumbled around in the porch, closing the door behind him and taking a few minutes to manage to lock it properly. As he was about to round the corner past the first apartment, which belonged to Jennifer and James, he noticed that the front door was open, indicating that Jennifer had clearly got over her most recent hissy fit and was duly rested from the early night.

The seven steps he'd already taken were more than enough, and facing much more of the sun right now was not an attractive proposition. He knocked on the door, hoping to see Jennifer or James and see what they had planned for the day. Anything was better than the sun. When no reply came, he poked his head inside the door and listened for the sound of running water or other generally bathroomy sounds which meant that he should beat a hasty and polite retreat. There was no sound at all.

He called out. 'Hello?'

Still no response.

Ellis pushed the door open a little further and saw that the bathroom door was also slightly ajar. For reasons completely unknown to him, he headed for the bathroom and pushed the door open. As the door thudded against something solid but soft, he stepped inside and recoiled in horror at what he saw: Jennifer's body hung limply over the side of the bath, her head lolled against the porcelain, her extremities blue.

13

Ellis's first instinct was to fetch Hardwick. Well, if truth be told his first instinct was to rid himself of the contents of his stomach, but yet again even the sight of a dead body was more appetising than alcohol right now.

He stumbled out of the apartment and back into the blinding sun, the world around him swerving and swaying in the heat, the alcohol sloshing around behind his eyes as he tried to make sense of his surroundings.

Knowing Hardwick wasn't in the apartment, and also knowing that he was prone to rising early, Ellis headed for the pool area. He had to stop a couple of times to steady himself and make sure he wasn't going to be ill.

He glanced over at the sun loungers. On seeing James, he turned as white as a sheet and said nothing, simply beckoning Hardwick over towards the bar area to speak to him more quietly.

'Christ, Ellis, you look like death warmed up,' Hardwick said, with a cheeky smile which told him that he was less than sympathetic.

'That's not so far from the truth. There's been a murder.'

'What?'

'A murder. Someone's been killed.'

'I know what a murder is, Ellis. I mean, how do you know? Are you sure this isn't just another one of your alcohol-induced dreams?'

'Yes, I'm sure! I just found her! Unless she's shoved her own head in a bath full of water and drowned herself, it's bloody murder, Kempston!'

'Ellis, calm down. What do you mean *her*? Who is it?'

'Jennifer!' Ellis said with the growl of a wild animal in his voice, despite not raising his voice much above a whisper.

'Where?'

'Her apartment,' Ellis replied, trying to swallow down the rising vomit. 'The door was open, so I called out but there was no answer, so I—'

'Open?'

'Yes,' Ellis replied. 'Only slightly, but enough that it was obvious.'

'Interesting. Find the owner, let him know what's happened. But don't tell anyone else. I'll meet you back at Jennifer's apartment.'

Hardwick headed in the direction of the apartment, deliberately not looking in James's direction as he passed him, sure that his eyes would betray him if he did so.

Ellis, meanwhile, found the closest bush and retched.

14

When Ellis had finally recovered and managed to find Stavros Giannakopoulos, the hotel's owner was visibly taken aback by what he had been told. His main concern, though, seemed to be financial.

Once Hardwick had established that Jennifer Alexander was, indeed, very much dead, he came to find Ellis and Stavros. His first thought was that Ellis seemed to be looking much better.

'This is terrible news,' Stavros said as Hardwick told him what had happened in apartment number one.

'Yes, it is. Please call the police and we'll let them deal with it,' Hardwick said, before turning to head for the door. Ellis shook his dead in disbelief, but Stavros beat him to speaking.

'No! Please, no police! I will lose everything! This place is all I have. I am almost bankrupt now anyway, and this will finish me!' he implored, his face pained at the prospect of what could be. His words had clearly had an effect on Ellis, who turned to Hardwick — someone who clearly had not been swayed at all.

'Kempston, surely we could...' Ellis started, before Stavros spoke again. Hardwick simply closed his eyes and sighed.

'The Kollidis has not made much money in years, not since the economy collapsed. Me and my family are hanging on, but we cannot lose our home and our life. Things will get better. The country will get better. But until then, we must hold on. If you call the police, they will close down the Kollidis and I will be finished! Please, Mr Hardwick. I know you are a detective. I have seen your name in the newspapers and all over the internet. You can help me. You can find out who did this and save my business also. Please.'

Hardwick thought for a moment. 'No. Sorry. I decided yesterday I was going to make the most of this holiday and I'm certainly not going to go around solving murders while I'm here. As far as I'm concerned, I'm off work for the week.'

'But you are the only person who can help me, Mr Hardwick! Please!' Stavros begged, by now on his knees in front of him, tears streaming down his face.

'Ellis has helped me in the past,' Hardwick said, doing his level best not to look the hotel owner in the eye, lest he cave. 'I'm sure he'd be able to offer his opinion and expertise. To the police.'

Ellis took Hardwick by the arm and pulled him aside.

'Before you say it, Ellis, *no*.'

'Kempston, just think about it. You're not thinking straight. Look at the man! If we call the police, his business will be ruined and his life will be over. How can you possibly consider doing that to a man?'

'Ellis, things have to be done through the proper channels.'

'And since when were you one for going through the proper channels?' Ellis half-whispered half-barked. 'It's never bothered you before, so don't you dare wheel that one out now. Now, I know you, Kempston. You're a good man and you know what's right. What's happened to your passion for justice?'

'It's in England, Ellis, and I'm not. Now let that be

an end to it,' Hardwick said, attempting to pull away from Ellis.

'No! I won't!' Ellis said, suddenly stepping his anger up a notch and pulling Hardwick in even closer. 'A young woman has died here and the person who killed her is going to get away scot free and this man's business and livelihood is going to collapse if you don't help. Do you really want that on your conscience?'

Kempston Hardwick, a man who had dedicated his life to doing good wherever possible, had been put into an impossible situation. He bowed his head and sighed heavily.

'Ellis, it wouldn't work. I can hardly imagine any of the holidaymakers would accept the notion of a murder having taken place, the police not being called and the two of us investigating it instead.'

'We've managed before,' Ellis replied.

'No, we have always worked *with* the police before. Or certainly at the same time as them, anyway,' Hardwick added, remembering that Detective Inspector Rob Warner of Tollinghill Police had not always been entirely keen on their "interference" as he put it.

'No! No police!' Stavros said, clearly agitated at the suggestion.

'No, you've already said,' Hardwick replied. 'But

we do have to find a way to make this credible. If — *if* — we do it.'

There was silence for a few moments before Stavros perked up again.

'I have an idea! I have a cousin who was in the Greek police. If I call him, he can come here and say that you are to investigate.'

Hardwick thought for a moment. 'Mr Giannakopoulos, when you say your cousin *was* a police officer, what do you mean exactly?'

'He was a police officer. Now he is not.'

'Yes, I understood that much. But why is he no longer a police officer?'

'Is a long story,' Stavros said, taking Hardwick by the arm. 'So tell me. You are in, yes?'

15

Hardwick sighed as he stood in the tiled bathroom and looked at the body of Jennifer Alexander. Her back was arched at an unnatural angle, her body folded over the edge of the bath. Her muscles would've relaxed after she'd died, and the human spine is a remarkably flexible piece of machinery when it isn't being held up by muscular tension and nerve feedback.

She looked like a rag doll, just carelessly flung over the side of the bath like a used towel. Dead bodies never looked particularly human, but Jennifer's looked even less so. The clean, tidy domestic surroundings of the bathroom seemed completely at odds with the reality of the situation — that a woman had died in here.

Her tousled hair clung to her arm like seaweed, her entire upper body inside the bath, save for her other arm, which was arched over the side. Her hair was bedraggled, but didn't look like it had been made wet by water, but rather by sweat. Hardwick very quickly ruled out drowning. He wasn't dismissive of the idea, though; he knew how much careless assumptions could affect a murder investigation. Indeed, the bruising around her neck seemed to indicate the true cause of death.

'Looks like she's been strangled,' Hardwick offered.

'With what?' Ellis asked, noting the bruising but still at a loss to explain exactly what had happened.

'Hard to say. A combination of things, by the looks of it. Could be hands here,' he said, pointing to an area on the upper half of her neck which had become mottled and bruised. 'But these marks here look like some sort of rope. Or this,' he said, picking up a white fluffy cord. 'Looks like the belt from the dressing gown on the back of the door.'

'The killer must have grabbed it as the closest thing at hand, so presumably she died in here,' Ellis said, proud of his deduction.

'So it seems. Rather a messy and fussy way to kill

someone, strangulation. Not the hallmark of a planned murder, if you ask me. If you're planning to kill someone you'd do it somewhere away from other people, perhaps with poisoning or something a little more definite and less risky. A tricky one to get away with, strangulation, especially in the middle of the night,' Hardwick said, manoeuvring to inspect the tiled walls and other aspects of the bathroom in a better light. He could see no blood, nor anything which would help identify the killer. Jennifer Alexander appeared to have put up, or been able to put up, very little of a struggle.

'You reckon it was a spur of the moment thing then?' Ellis asked.

'I'd say so. No forced entry, so Jennifer must have known her killer — or at least known who they were, else she wouldn't have let them in voluntarily. Don't forget that she wouldn't even open the door to her fiancé a few hours earlier. And it doesn't look as though anything has been stolen, either. Her mobile phone and purse are in plain sight on the dresser and her handbag wasn't far from the door, so I think we can rule out robbery as a motive. Notice anything else odd?'

'You mean apart from the fact there's a dead

woman lumped over the side of her bath?' Ellis replied facetiously.

'Yes, Ellis,' Hardwick said, ignoring Ellis's sarcasm. 'She's still wearing the dress she had on last night. Which means she hadn't gone to bed by the time her killer arrived.'

'That doesn't mean a thing,' Ellis said. 'I quite often sit up watching some TV when I get in from a night out. Maybe that's what Jennifer did. Or maybe she read a book or just sat about for a bit, waiting for James to get back.'

'Ellis, she kicked him out for the night. She wasn't waiting for anyone.'

'Well, maybe she'd had a bit too much to drink then. A few times I've fallen asleep fully clothed after a night on the tiles.'

'That doesn't surprise me one bit, Ellis. But from the very little I saw of Jennifer Alexander, I wouldn't have put her down as the type of person who would fall asleep fully clothed. It's possible, but to me it points to her killer having struck sooner rather than later.'

Hardwick took a step back and examined the bathroom with a wider viewing angle. Sometimes, he knew, you could be a little too close to see what was actually happening, or had happened. The old maxim that sometimes you just can't see the wood for the trees was a very true one.

'Ellis, you're going to have to help me round up everybody who's staying here at the moment. We're going to need to speak to everyone. Without being able to get the police involved we're going to have to use logic, deduction and our own noses. Ah. And time.'

'Time?' Ellis asked, his brain still pounding from the previous night's excesses.

'Indeed. James, Darryl and Alicia leave for home in a few days' time, as do the others who were here for a fortnight and had already had a week here. That gives us only a few days to find our killer.'

16

Spiros Stephanidis looked much the same as his cousin, Stavros, but with a decidedly shiftier air about him. He embraced Stavros with a very manly hug and a kiss on each cheek as he arrived some half an hour after his cousin's phone call.

Hardwick spoke some Greek, but the odd local dialect and slang which Stavros and Spiros were speaking made much of it completely incomprehensible.

The introductions and formalities having been got out of the way, Hardwick, Flint and the two cousins made their way to the pool bar, where the holiday-makers had been asked to assemble following the news of Jennifer Alexander's death.

Spiros was straight into police officer mode, clearly relishing his lost years since he had last worked as a detective.

'Good morning. I am Police Lieutenant Stephanidis,' he said, his chest pushed out proudly.

Hardwick raised one eyebrow slightly, sure that any attentive person would've realised that the Greek police force no longer used the old military-style titles, but that his equivalent rank would now be referred to as Chief Inspector.

'I am sure that you will now all know — Miss Jennifer Alexander was murdered in her room at some point last night.'

'*Murdered?*' Alicia said as her hand shot to her mouth.

'Yes, I am sorry,' Spiros said. 'And this is now a murder investigation. Because the police force on Friktos is quite small, and because we do not speak good English,' he said in perfect English, 'we have authorised these two gentleman from England, who are both—'

'Detectives,' Hardwick butted in before Spiros could say *police officers*. Even when — in legal terms — covering up a murder and desecrating the evidence in order to do a failing businessman a favour, Hardwick was still unable to be anything other than honest, even if it meant being honest in his own inimitable way.

'Yes. These gentlemen will speak to you all and ask what you remember from last night. Anything you can remember will help to find the killer of Miss Alexander. The information they receive,' Spiros lied, 'will be passed to our detectives in order to try to find out what happened.'

'And what are we meant to do?' Nick Roder asked, already cradling a pint of lager. 'Just sit around and wait? Go home? Get on with our holiday?'

'I ask only that you co-operate with the Detectives Hardwick and Flint and help them as they see fit. Unless you are suspected of a crime and arrested for it, we cannot keep you on the island or in the country. But thankfully the European Union means that we can also pursue suspects if they decide to go home. In the meantime, if you do not have a guilty conscience you can do as you please.'

Nick Roder took a large gulp of lager.

'So. Does anybody have any questions?' Spiros asked.

'I do,' Nick said. 'Can I buy you a drink?'

17

It occurred to Hardwick that he needed to be certain of who was in the apartment complex the previous evening and overnight. His first port of call was to visit the reception desk to see if any unknown visitors had been noticed.

The hotel owner's daughter, Maria, was as helpful as her demeanour allowed, and she explained to Hardwick and Flint that they had a number of security measures in place which would have made it almost impossible for a stranger to enter the complex.

'Nobody can enter a room which is not theirs,' she said, matter-of-factly. 'The doors do not open from the outside without a key, and there is only one key per room. The keys are kept here at the reception desk —

that is our policy — so they are not lost outside. If someone is outside of the hotel and comes in, they must come here to collect their key first.'

Hardwick pursed his lips. That made two things impossible — that the killer had used his or her own key to go into the apartment that Jennifer was in, either before or after she got there herself. It left only one possibility — the one that made no sense — that she willingly opened the door and let her killer in.

'Also there is only one way in from outside the hotel complex, and that is the main entrance here,' Maria added. 'There is a security camera on this entrance at all times.'

'Does it record?' Hardwick asked.

'Yes, of course,' was the reply. 'My father has the recordings in his office.'

* * *

Hardwick certainly wouldn't have called the room an office; it was far too disorganised and messy for his liking. *Tidy house, tidy mind* was the maxim he followed. Now, as Stavros Giannakopoulos ran through the CCTV camera footage on his computer, Hardwick was struggling to maintain proper focus.

'So you see camera on entrance to complex here. We can see who is in or out at the time.'

'Is that the only way in or out of the complex?' Ellis Flint asked.

'Absolutely, yes. No other way.'

'And nobody else came in at all during the night?'

'No. On reception also we ask guests to deposit keys when they leave complex, for security. It is also for risk of fire, so we know at all times who is in hotel.'

'Right. So the only people in the complex, and therefore the only possible killers, are James Garfield, Darryl Potts, Alicia French, Nick Roder, Paul Erenson, Ryan Farley, Hayley Saunders, Emma Benson and Arjun Beqiri. Oh, and... well, myself, Kempston and yourself.'

'Yes. And also my daughter Maria, who works on reception desk.'

'Thirteen suspects,' Ellis said, glancing over at Hardwick, who seemed to be oblivious to the numerical significance.

'Are there any more CCTV cameras, Mr Giannakopoulos?' Hardwick asked, his eyes glazing over slightly.

'No,' came the reply after a short pause.

'So why does your software say "Camera 1 of 2"?'

Hardwick asked, pointing casually to the text in the bottom right-hand corner of the computer screen.

'Ah. Yes,' came Stavros's reply as he sheepishly moused down on the "Next camera" button. The screen changed to show a different camera with a different view.

'It's pointed at the sun loungers, Mr Giannakopoulos,' Hardwick said with no emotion in his voice.

'Yes. Is for security.'

'Against what possible misdemeanours, might I ask? Unsuitable iPod covers? Over-application of suntan lotion? Or could it possibly be that it's the area that scantily-clad female holidaymakers tend to spend large portions of the day?'

The embarrassed owner said nothing.

'Fortunately enough,' Hardwick continued, 'that might just help us quite a bit more than you might think. I presume the camera switches to infrared at nighttime?'

'Of course.'

'So you could see the sun-loungers on this camera quite clearly throughout the night?'

'Yes.'

'Right. Could you skip the footage to twelve-thirty this morning, please?'

Stavros did as he was told and the footage began to play, showing nothing but empty sun loungers for a couple of minutes. Before long, the distinctive figures of Hardwick and James Garfield entered the shot, with James lying down on the sun lounger in a foetal position, Hardwick appearing to wish him a good night. Seconds later, Hardwick left the shot in the direction of the apartment block.

'Can you forward it on at a faster speed?' Hardwick asked Stavros.

As the time sped up, the trio watched James on the sun lounger, completely still except for the occasional toss or turn. As the light began to rise, the camera switched from infrared to daytime mode and Arjun entered the shot with his pool net as Stavros returned the footage to normal speed.

'So James Garfield stayed on the sun lounger all night.'

'Yep. And he was still there by the time I'd found Jennifer dead,' Ellis said as the footage clearly began to show Hardwick being approached by Ellis early that morning. 'Which rules him out, then, as the apartment door was locked when he went to sleep and only open again when he woke up. On the sun lounger, where he'd been all night.'

'Indeed,' Hardwick said. 'Just one last thing for now, Mr Giannakopoulos. Where do you keep your accounting records?'

'Accounting? I hate it. All paperwork goes from reception to my accountant in the main town. He takes care of everything.'

Satisfied, Hardwick led Ellis Flint from Stavros Giannakopoulous's office and they headed in the direction of the pool bar.

'What have the accounts got to do with anything, Hardwick?' Ellis asked innocently.

'Last night when he left the pool bar he said he was going to his office to do some accounting work. But he just told us he doesn't do his own accounts. All he has in his office is a computer for monitoring his CCTV footage. Of the main entrance. And the sun loungers.'

'So when he came back to his office last night to do his accounts...'

'Let's leave it there, shall we, Ellis? It doesn't bear thinking about. I've just had my breakfast.'

18

Fortunately, Arjun had deemed that a brutal murder was just about cause enough to not have dance music pumping out through the speakers and cocktails lined up on the bar. Instead, he was in his second of two very different modes — his go-slow mode, which consisted of reclining back on his stool and playing on his mobile phone.

James was sat at a table by the pool bar, his elbow on the table and his head resting on his hand, staring into the middle distance when Hardwick and Flint arrived. His eyes looked red raw, his face a picture of disbelief at what had happened.

'James, is it all right if we ask you a few questions?' Ellis said, getting in early before Hardwick could say something insensitive. 'Kempston and I are detectives — of sorts — and the hotel manager has asked us to look into what happened to Jennifer.'

'Uh... yes, fine,' James replied, seemingly in another world entirely, struggling to comprehend what had happened. 'Shouldn't the tourism police be doing this, though? I thought they were there to help tourists. I'm still not quite sure I understand '

'They're... on strike,' Ellis replied, thinking far more quickly than he should have been, considering his raging hangover.

'Yes, and they don't tend to deal with murders,' Hardwick added, truthfully. 'More commercial disputes.'

'Oh. I just... I just can't believe it. She was fine earlier in the evening. Well, I mean, she wasn't fine, but at least she wasn't...'

'Yes. I know,' Hardwick replied. 'And I'm sorry to remind you of it, but we really do need to get everything straight. I know a lot happened and it can be difficult to remember, but you really do need to try to be as accurate as possible, so that we can get all of the information together and find out what happened to your fiancée. At what time did you leave the bar?'

'Um, around a quarter to eleven, I think.'

'Can you be a little more specific?' Hardwick asked.

'Not really. You were there too. I wasn't really watching the clock. I think Jennifer went back to the room at about half ten, and I probably stayed at the bar for another ten or fifteen minutes or so after that.'

'And what happened when you got back to the apartment?'

'The door was locked. The reception only gives you one key when you check in, and Jennifer had that one. I banged on the door for her to let me in, but she just shouted back at me and said she wasn't going to. Something about having been embarrassed and shown up in front of everyone. There was clearly no reasoning with her. There never is when she's in that sort of mood. So I came back to the bar.'

'Did anyone see you while you were outside the apartment?'

'Um... Yeah, Darryl did, actually. He came out of his apartment to see what all the noise was about.'

'And then he went back into his own apartment?'

'Yeah. After he stood and watched me walk all the way back to the bar. Bloke's got a screw loose.'

'So if we ask him, he'd tell us the same thing? That

the door was locked, Jennifer didn't let you in and he watched you all the way back to the bar?'

'Well, I'd bloody hope so. Only problem is, I can't stand him and he isn't exactly my biggest fan either, so I wouldn't put it past him to try and stitch me up.'

Hardwick thought for a few moments before asking another question.

'Did you have life insurance out on your fiancée at all?' he asked.

Very tactful, Ellis thought. James's face seemed to show much the same thought.

'No. No, I didn't. We would've needed it had we bought a house, but we were just renting until we'd got the wedding out of the way.'

'And how long had you lived together for?' Hardwick followed up.

'Just under a year. So no, common-law rules don't kick in either. I'm entitled to nothing out of her death. I benefit in absolutely no way at all. Happy now?'

19

Darryl Potts seemed visibly shocked when he was told the news about Jennifer. He was still in his apartment, tending to the unwell Alicia when they'd knocked on the door of apartment 2. Fortunately, Alicia seemed to be looking a little bit brighter and Darryl was happy to join Hardwick and Flint at a table near the bar.

Hardwick had asked him, too, what his version of events was for the previous evening.

'It was about ten o'clock, I think, Alicia said she wasn't feeling great so I escorted her back to the room. I wanted to make sure she was asleep and not going to be ill, because I thought it might just be a bit of sunstroke and too much to drink. So I sat and read some of my book for about half an hour or so, just to make sure she was all right before I thought about maybe heading back to the bar. Next thing I know, I can hear James banging on his door — they're in the apartment next to us — and I can hear him and Jennifer arguing about something. He was asking her to let him in, but she wouldn't. I went out to see what all the fuss was about, and I asked her to let me in, but she wouldn't do that either. She said she didn't want to see anyone until the morning. So James went back to the bar and I went back into my apartment.'

'Did you see him go all the way back to the bar?' Hardwick asked.

'Oh yes, I made sure of it. Watched him the whole way. I didn't want him coming back and upsetting Jennifer any more. It was best for everyone that she just slept it off and woke up in the morning as if nothing ever happened. Like she always did.'

'And Alicia can vouch for all of this?' Ellis asked.

'Yeah, the banging woke her up. She didn't get back to sleep properly again after that, either, so she can vouch for the fact that I was in bed all night from then.'

'She was awake all night?' Hardwick asked.

'Yeah. She was in quite a lot of pain, had a migraine and felt really unwell. I think she's OK now, just sleeping it off. I was awake most of the night as well, as I couldn't sleep knowing she was in pain. Hence being in bed so late this morning.'

'And did you hear anything else after James went back to the bar?'

'No, not really. That's the amazing thing. You'd think if someone was strangled to death in the room next to you, you'd hear something, wouldn't you?'

'I should imagine so. And surely you would have heard if someone had knocked on the door, too?'

'Ah, well that depends. I heard James banging on the door earlier in the night because it was so quiet and he was banging so loudly. Later on I watched a bit of TV, so that might have scuppered things a bit in terms of hearing things. And someone going to commit murder probably wouldn't knock as loudly as James did.'

'I see,' Hardwick said. 'On the subject of James Garfield, would it be fair to say that you and he don't exactly see eye to eye on a lot of things?'

'In a word, yes.' Darryl said, his face dropping. 'I can't stand the bloke.'

'Any particular reason why?'

'Many. Mainly he just doesn't like me, and kind of rubs me up the wrong way because of that. He's always making snide comments and we just don't get on. Simple as that.'

'And Jennifer? Did you get on with her?'

'Yeah, I did. I think I was one of the only people who did, apart from Alicia,' Darryl said, with a slight chuckle.

'So do you think there's any chance James Garfield could have killed his fiancée?'

'James? Christ, no. I mean, they bickered like any couple but that's just how they were. Jennifer was a vamp and James is just quiet and mouse-like. That's probably part of the reason we don't get on. I'm far more confident and outgoing, and he probably just thinks I'm loud and brash or something. Personally, I find him boring. Not a bloody murderer, though. As much as I don't particularly like him, even I'd draw the line there.'

Hardwick nodded and logged this all in his memory whilst Ellis Flint scribbled furiously in his notebook, not able to rely on a colossal memory as Hardwick was.

'As much as I'd love to see James banged up in some Greek prison cell, I'm not going to lie — I'm certain he couldn't have done it.'

20

Nick Roder had a rather casual demeanour — one which tended to rile Hardwick in situations such as this, in which someone had died. He seemed to have more to say about his sexual conquests with Hayley Saunders than he did about the fact that someone's life had been violently taken from them.

Before they'd got down to the business of constructing the night's events with him, Nick had been far more concerned as to whether he was going to get to eat at some point. Arjun had very delicately tried to explain that there would be no food available for the foreseeable future because the cold store was unfortunately out of action, being temporarily used for other purposes. Nick wasn't particularly happy about this, but didn't ask for an elaboration. That was pretty fortunate, Hardwick thought, as the cold store was being temporarily used for the purpose of storing Jennifer Alexander's corpse.

Hardwick probed Nick on the subject of Hayley Saunders, hoping to find out some information which might lead him and Flint in the direction of some sort of motive for murder. Instead, Nick was remarkably casual about the whole affair.

'It's just a casual thing, like,' he said, leaning back on the chair with his arm hooked over the back and one leg crossed over the other. 'Just a group of lads and birds on holiday, and that sort of thing happens don't it? They come over on the same flight as us and turns out we was all staying at the same place, so we got chatting. Nothing serious.'

'I guessed that when I watched you trying to chat up Jennifer Alexander,' Hardwick said, noting that Nick's face twitched slightly at hearing her name.

'Yeah, well, that's life ain't it? Some you win, some you don't.'

'Did it not seem to bother you at all that she was there with her fiancé?'

'Nah, not really. He seems like a bit of a drip anyway so thought it was worth a shot. Sort of thing that happens after a few drinks. No harm in it, is there?'

Hardwick decided not to respond to that question.

'What makes you think that way about James?' Ellis asked.

'Well come on, you must have noticed it yourself. The bloke's a mouse. No harm in livening him up a bit, is there? Bringing him out of his shell, like.'

Hardwick gritted his teeth and got straight to the point. 'Mr Roder, you were the first of your group to go back to your apartment that night, yes?'

'Yeah, what of it?'

'Well, you were gone a whole fifty-five minutes before Paul and Ryan went back to the apartment. What were you doing in that time?'

'Uh, sleeping, funnily enough,' he answered in a mocking tone of voice. 'Sorry, but I wasn't busy bludgeoning some old bird to death if that's what you're thinking.'

'Mr Roder, when you went back to your apartment, you made a comment to your friends. You said "Don't worry, lads, I'll get my bit". What did that mean?'

'Just one of those stupid things you say, you know?'

Hardwick was incensed, and he sprang up from his

chair and put his face just inches away from Nick's, his eyes fierce with anger in a rare display of emotion.

'No. No, I do not know. But to me it sounds very much like a death threat. A death threat made to a woman just hours before she was murdered. That makes you a bloody strong suspect. So why don't you tell me *exactly* what it meant?'

Nick stayed silent for a few moments, finding it hard to judge Hardwick accurately after his outburst.

'Look, it was a stupid thing to say, OK? It wasn't a threat. I'd just had a few drinks and I thought it was funny. How was I meant to know she was going to get bloody murdered?'

Hardwick now spoke calmly and clearly. 'That's exactly what I intend to find out, Mr Roder.'

21

Hardwick, Flint and Paul Erenson sat down at the table in Costas's Taverna on the outskirts of the town. By now, Hardwick was getting pretty pig sick of the bar area at the apartment complex and wanted to benefit from new surroundings. It was Paul who had suggested they head to Costas's, as they'd eaten there a few times over the past week.

'The beer's good here,' Paul said, as the waiter came to take their drinks order. 'One of the only ones in town that serves the local brew on draught rather than in bottles. Always tastes better that way, I reckon.'

Ellis Flint nodded his agreement, but decided to pass on the alcohol. He wasn't entirely sure he could ever drink again. Although Paul was opting for hair of the dog, Hardwick and Flint both opted for black coffee.

'How do you and your friends know each other?' Hardwick asked.

'I used to go to school with Nick. Well, sixth-form, anyway. We were in the same Media Studies group. We met Ryan when we used to play five-a-side football down at the local pitches on a Tuesday night. He'd come on the wrong night — used to play on Wednesdays — and we were a player short that night so he played for us anyway. Been hanging around with him ever since.'

'What about Hayley and Emma?'

'Ah, we don't really know them at all. Only met them here, and spent a few nights hanging around with them. They're a good laugh, and we've been to a couple of clubs and that. Nothing serious. Nick had been having a bit of a thing with Hayley, but that's just one of them holiday romances, you know? Sort of thing that always happens.'

'I'll get straight to the point,' Hardwick said, 'Can you think of any reason why anyone at the apartment complex would want to kill Jennifer Alexander?'

Paul thought for a few moments. 'Well, yes. But I don't think that any of them would be reasons to actually do it. I mean, she pissed off quite a few people. She was one of those people who speaks her mind, you know? Wouldn't be afraid to tell you if she thought you was a tosser. Wouldn't be enough to make you kill someone, though, would it?'

'The amount some people had had to drink, it probably wouldn't have taken much,' Ellis offered.

'True,' Paul replied. 'But even then, you'd just say something or start a barney, wouldn't you? You wouldn't go into her apartment and strangle the bird to death. That's madness, that is.'

'Am I right in thinking you share an apartment with your two friends?' Hardwick asked, changing the subject slightly.

'Yeah, that's right. Ryan and Nick. Got one of those family apartments with two rooms, a double and a twin. We spun for the double and Nick got it. Made fair use of it, too,' he said, laughing.

'And you sleep in the twin room with Ryan?' Ellis asked.

'Yeah. That's right,' Paul replied, his voice quieter than it had been.

'Did you go back to the apartment together on the night Jennifer died?' Hardwick asked.

'Yeah, we all did. Ellis came back at the same time so can vouch for us.'

Ellis nodded his agreement as he took a sip of his coffee, which had since arrived.

'And you all stayed there until the morning?'

Paul went silent for a few moments, sighing quietly, something clearly on his mind.

'It's probably nothing, but I should tell you anyway. Ryan always gets up early. Force of habit I think, because he has to get up so early for work when he's at home. He got up at about five-thirty and went out of the apartment for about five minutes. I heard him, because my bed's nearest the door. I'm a light sleeper, so I hear all sorts of things. I can see the main door into the apartment from there, too, and I saw him go.'

'I see. And did he say where he was going?' Hardwick asked.

'No, I asked him when he came back. Said he went to see what time breakfast started.'

Hardwick knew from memory that there was a large chalkboard in the reception area which stated in large white letters that breakfast started at seven o'clock. 'And did he manage to find out?'

'No, he said he couldn't find anyone to ask.'

Hardwick tried his level best not to make any sort of facial movement. 'I apologise in advance, Mr Erenson, but I need to ask you a very direct question. Do you know of any reason why Ryan Farley might want to have killed Jennifer Alexander?'

'Christ, no. None at all. He barely knew her. None of us did. To be honest, Ryan's a pretty quiet guy. I really can't imagine him doing anything like that at all. I've known him for a few years and he'd barely say boo to a goose, never mind anything more than that. Well...' Paul said as his voice trailed off.

'Yes?' said Hardwick.

'Well, they always say, don't they — that it's often the quiet ones you need to watch out for.'

22

Hayley Saunders seemed apparently oblivious to the severity of the situation, instead having gone into an extensive monologue on how she first knew Emma Benson, the various boyfriends they'd had, their relationship with their respective parents and the previous holidays they'd been on together. Lively and talkative seemed to be two words which described Hayley very well.

'We was always best mates at school, though. Our parents was mates too, and we used to go on holiday together and that. Sorta carried it on when we got older and that, we go somewhere every year. Done Kavos, Magaluf, Malia, now Kakagoustos. Gotta say, it's right up there, innit? Some wicked clubs and people here are well nice.'

Hardwick attempted to interrupt, but Hayley was on a roll.

'I mean, we went to Malia and the people there was a bit funny, you know? Got a bad name for itself there now. Mostly where the kids go when they ain't got a clue where the best places are now. Bit too much mess there now.'

Hardly a blissful paradise here, either, Hardwick thought.

'Places like Ibiza and Kavos are getting a bit expensive 'n all. People cotton on to what's popular and all the prices go up, know what I mean? Might as well have a week in Newcastle for half the price of what it costs to go to Magaluf now. Ain't got the sun, of course, but that ain't everything is it? Not if you just wanna have a good time and get a few drinks down ya and meet some new people.'

'So can you talk us through what happened on Monday night, please?' Ellis finally asked, sensing that Hardwick was about to make some sort of flippant remark if the conversation wasn't brought to a point very quickly.

'Monday?' she said, as if the significance of that

particular night was completely lost on her. 'Well we went out into town for some food, but we went pretty early. Gotta get in before the crowds, ain't ya? We went down to that Giorgio's, you know it? Italian place, I think. They do a right lovely pasta carbonara down there, and it ain't too creamy either, so good for the diet. If you ask them nicely, they'll even do it with wholewheat pasta so you ain't got all the starchy carbs and that, too. They do some cracking pizzas, but can be a bit heavy if you're havin' a night out, you know what I mean? Don't wanna be feeling all bloated 'n that, do ya?'

'Right. I meant more about what happened when you got back to the pool bar, actually.'

'Oh right, yeah. Well we got back pretty early. Fancied having a night at the pool bar and then having a proper big night out the next day. We walked up to the bar and ordered our drinks. I had a mojito and I think Emma had a Black Russian or something like that. Might've been a White Russian, actually. Which one's the one with Tia Maria in it? Probably a Black Russian, then, cos Tia Maria's quite dark, innit? That's the coffee one, yeah? Yeah. Well anyway, we had them and then we went and sat down at one of the tables. Was that one with the wicker bench, what they put near the pool. It's proper nice there in the evenings, cos the breeze comes off the pool and cools you down a bit. Best thing in a heatwave, that. The boys come and sat with us a bit later when they got back, like, and we had some more drinks — I think I had a couple of Jäger-bombs actually, and—'

'The boys? You mean Paul, Nick and Ryan?'

'Yeah, that's them. I dunno if you've spoke to them yet, but basically me and Nick had this bit of a thing going on, but I think he's just here on a lads' holiday so he's just taking what he can get, if you know what I mean. All the bloody same, if you ask me.' Ellis didn't, but she told him anyway. 'I mean, surely you'd try and hide it or something? But no, he just walks straight up to her, this Jennifer bird, and starts chatting her up! Right in front of me! I reckon he did it to try and put me off or something, but it ain't gonna work. Point of principle, innit? I mean, I've 'ad blokes like that before, what try and do all this treatin' mean keepin' keen stuff, but I ain't fallin' for that. Plenty more fish in the sea, ain't there? Specially in a place like this!' she said, putting her hand briefly on Ellis's knee.

'And did you speak to Nick about it at the time?' Hardwick asked.

'Too bloody right I did! Give him a right earful. Ain't the way to treat a lady, is it?'

Ellis said nothing about the misappropriation of the word "lady" and let Hayley have her moment of glory. 'And what about overnight? Did either you or Emma leave your room? I mean, can you vouch for her whereabouts all night?'

'Nah. At least, I didn't go nowhere anyway. We got up about ten this morning and left the room about half past. Can't really say much about overnight, though, cos I'm a heavy sleeper a the best of times. After the amount I had to drink that night, I wouldn't've heard a bomb go off. Talkin' of bombs, have you tried them new Glitterbomb things? It's like energy drink, right, but with this glittery stuff which...'

23

Having finally managed to extricate themselves from Hayley's presence, Hardwick reflected that this was the only time he'd had to feign illness to get someone to stop talking. Usually, it was the other way round: it was more than enough trouble trying to get witnesses to talk in the first place. This was very much the case with Emma Benson, who sat and twirled curls of her blonde hair around her finger as Hardwick and Flint asked for her recollection of the events that occurred on the night Jennifer Alexander died.

'We went up to bed about midnight. Most people had gone by then so the atmosphere had pretty much died, and it was only the boys left, so I suggested we got an early night,' she said. Hardwick wondered how she'd managed to get a word in edgeways that evening, having been sat with Hayley Saunders. 'Hayley's been seeing that Nick bloke, but I don't really like them. I mean, Ryan's all right — he's a bit quieter — but Nick and Paul can be a bit... brash.'

'Do you not get on with brash people?' Ellis asked, tactfully.

'Not really, no. I prefer to relax on my holidays, not have to listen to people barking on at me.'

Kempston Hardwick was not quite as tactful. 'Do you not think Hayley is a bit... well, brash?'

Emma's head snapped upwards to meet Hardwick's gaze for the first time.

'Hayley is not brash.'

'Well, I mean, she's pretty lively and talkative,' Hardwick expanded, a little shocked at Emma's sudden change of character.

'She's kind and caring, is Hayley. All right, yes, sometimes she likes to talk but what's the harm in that? She's a bloody good friend, and that's the main thing,' she said, holding Hardwick's gaze.

'I don't think Kempston meant to case aspersions on your friendship,' Ellis said. 'I think he just meant that—'

'I don't care what he meant. Hayley's a good person, all right?'

Finally, she broke eye contact with Hardwick and resumed twiddling her hair with one hand, whilst picking at the middle fingernail of her other hand with its thumb.

'So you were with Hayley the whole night?' Hardwick asked after a few moments' silence.

'Yes. We spent the evening together and we share an apartment.'

'And she didn't leave the apartment during the night?' Ellis asked.

'What the hell would she do that for? Hayley's not the sort to just disappear off for midnight walks. That'd just be weird.'

'No, but can you be sure that she didn't?'

'I don't need to be. She's not that type of person. But to answer your question, no. I'm a pretty heavy sleeper and not much wakes me up, to be honest. But like I said, it's irrelevant. Hayley's not like that.'

* * *

Having realised they weren't really getting anywhere with Emma Benson, Hardwick and Flint reconvened at a local bar to grab some lunch.

'Bit odd that she was so defensive over Hayley, wasn't it?' Ellis asked with a mouthful of tzatziki.

'Indeed. That could be for any number of reasons, though. Doesn't necessarily make it anything suspicious, Ellis.'

'No, but that kind of blind defensiveness was just weird. She wouldn't even entertain the idea of Hayley having left the apartment, never mind anything else. Do you reckon she might know something?'

'Impossible to say at this stage,' Hardwick said, spreading a thick paste of hummus onto his bread. 'I wouldn't go getting too unduly worried. She didn't really raise too much suspicion in me, and I'm usually pretty good at telling when someone's being deceptive.'

'Well aren't you the modern-day Hercule Poirot?' Ellis said, with more than a hint of sarcasm.

'Certainly not,' Hardwick replied. 'The man was a sociopath.'

Ellis stared open-eyed at Hardwick, not wanting to say anything, but making his words perfectly clear through his eyes.

'Did you know that Agatha Christie hated Poirot?'

Hardwick said. 'She called him a detestable, bombastic, tiresome, ego-centric little creep. I can't say I blame her.'

'I can't imagine a writer thinking that about one of their own characters. Doesn't quite ring true to me.'

'Oh, I can assure you it is,' Hardwick said, smiling as he popped his hummus-laden pita into his mouth.

The barman sidled over and asked if the pair wanted another round of drinks. Hardwick, not one to speak with his mouth full, simply nodded and the barman poured another Campari and orange and a pint of lager.

'Tell me,' Hardwick said when the barman returned. 'Are there many cultural sites to visit around the island? Perhaps something historical, mythological?'

'Kempston, don't you think we're a bit busy to be—' Ellis interjected, but he was met with Hardwick's raised palm and the barman's answer.

'Yes, there is a site in the mountains, where they have found many artefacts from ancient times. It has some links with Zeus, in fact,' the barman said, Hardwick's face displaying some look of relief and pleasure for the first time that week. 'You can get there by taxi. My brother is taxi driver, he can do good deal on the price for you if you say Theo sent you. That is me — Theo.'

'Pleased to meet you, Theo,' Hardwick said, extending his hand. 'I'm Kempston and this is Ellis.'

'Pleased to meet you, too. These are not names I have seen before — Kempston and Ellis. Are they common in England?'

'Not really, no,' Ellis replied. 'Is Theo popular in Greece?'

'Quite popular, yes. It means "God appearing". Is short for Theofanis. Not many people shorten to Theo. In Greece is usually shortened to Fani. But when I started working here with English tourists, they tell me is not such a good name.'

Hardwick and Flint struggled to stifle their laughter.

'Tell your brother,' Hardwick said, the Campari having gone to his head and made him giggle and speak a little higher-pitched than usual, 'that we would very much like for him to take us to see the artefacts. Perhaps later this week?'

'Yes, that is perfect,' Theo replied.

24

Alicia French was a quiet, unassuming type. Hardwick had often noted that it was usually that type of person who tended to end up attached to a louder, brasher partner. That could certainly be said of Alicia and Darryl as well as James and Jennifer. Hardwick admired the soft freckles under her eyes as she spoke, her voice subdued and gentle.

'I was feeling pretty rough, so I went to bed early. Darryl came back with me and sat with me for a while to make sure I was all right. The next thing I know, I can hear banging and shouting from James and Jennifer's room. By the time I woke up, Darryl had already gone to see what was going on.'

'You say you heard shouting?' Hardwick asked. 'What exactly did you hear?'

'I couldn't really make out the words,' she replied, looking slightly disappointed with herself. 'Although I did hear Jennifer say that she felt like she'd been embarrassed and shown up in front of everyone. That she felt stupid.'

'Interesting,' Hardwick said. 'Shown up how?'

'I don't know. I couldn't really hear what was going on. I presume she was angry because James left her on her own and she got pestered by that Nick bloke.'

'How long was Darryl out of the room for?' Ellis asked.

'I don't know. He'd already gone out by the time I realised what was happening. Can't have been long. He said James was banging on the door and she wouldn't let him in, so he told James to leave it and go back to the bar.'

'And did he?'

'Yeah, Darryl watched him go. Think he wanted to make sure he wasn't going to go making any more noise, because I wasn't feeling great.'

'And did you get back to sleep after that?' Hardwick asked.

'Not properly, no. I was awake for most of the

night. That's probably why I feel so tired now. Sorry, I'm sure I'm not being much help to you in this state.'

'You're being very helpful, I can assure you,' Hardwick said. 'So if you barely slept that night, can you say with some certainty that Darryl didn't leave the room?'

'Yes, definitely. I would've heard. When he came back in he didn't want to go back to the bar any more, so he locked the door and put the key in the drawer next to me. He's pretty security-conscious,' she said, smiling. 'One of his better attributes. He always makes me feel safe.'

'And can you think of anyone staying here who would've wanted to harm Jennifer? Had she fallen out with anyone?' Ellis asked.

'Oh, she was always falling out with people. A lot of people didn't really get her. I've known Jennifer for years, so I know that deep down she's a nice person. She's just a bit arrogant and stuff sometimes. I think it's a defensive thing, so she doesn't have to show her real emotions. I'm not really one for conflict, so most of it kind of went over my head, but she did have a knack of upsetting people. She'd only been here half a day, though — I can't imagine anyone would've killed her over some petty argument!'

'You'd be surprised the things that can cause an

unhinged person to commit murder, Miss French,' Hardwick said. What about in your party? Did any of you particularly dislike Jennifer?'

'No, not at all. I've been friends with her since I was a little girl, and James and Jennifer had a very strong relationship. They were inseparable. Darryl can't stand James, but gets on fine with Jennifer. I can't imagine for one minute it was any of them.'

25

Ellis sat down to speak to Ryan Farley, having left Hardwick to ask some further questions to Alicia. Once he'd finished, he planned to have another quick chat with Darryl Potts.

Ryan, for his quiet demeanour, seemed like a man who took great care over his appearance. He clearly looked after his body, being one of those irritating people who could get away with wearing tight t-shirts wherever he went without having to worry about a bulging belly protruding from underneath. This was not a state of physicality Ellis Flint was in.

Ryan seemed to be the only person not yet drinking alcohol that afternoon, instead opting for "mocktails", a selection of non-alcoholic cocktails which tasted far more sweet and sickly than the traditional cocktails. At least those ones had the benefit of an alcoholic kick.

'I met Nick and Paul by mistake, really,' he said. 'Was a couple of years ago now. I used to play five-a-side football on a Wednesday night for a team called Avington 'Arriers. I'd just started working where I am now, at a warehouse, and the hours had mucked me up a bit. I do six days on, two days off, so my weekends tend to shift back a day each week. Really buggered me up at first, and I turned up on the Tuesday instead of the Wednesday.

'Anyway, Nick and Paul, they played for a team called The Howlermen, and one of their lads hadn't turned up that night so they asked if I wanted to play for them. I enjoyed it more than I did with the other lads, so I ended up playing with them every week and that was that.'

'Must be tough work, in a warehouse,' Ellis probed. 'Must mean getting up early.'

'Oh yeah, definitely. I'm usually up at five-thirty, out the house by six and at work for six-thirty for a seven o'clock start. I like to get there a bit early and relax for half an hour, you know? Otherwise by the time you've started running around you've already been at it for an hour or so getting ready and stuff in the morning.'

'You must find it hard to get up later on your days off, I'd imagine?' Ellis asked.

'Yeah, I do. Even here I'm up early. I think it's the strong sun. What with the time difference, when we first got here I was waking up about an hour after we went to bed. It's not too bad now, though. More like five or six or something.'

'I see. And do you tend to stay in bed or get up?'

'I tend to stay in bed if I can. Not much point getting up too early round here, as no-one else bothers.'

'And what about the morning Jennifer Alexander was found?' Ellis asked. 'Did you stay in bed that morning?'

'I don't remember, to be honest,' Ryan said, seeming to think for a moment. 'Probably, yeah.'

'Only your friend, Paul, says you got up and left the apartment at about five-thirty that morning.'

Ryan sat silently for a few moments, his face turning a shade of pink as he realised the implications.

'Yeah. That morning. Yeah. Yeah, I couldn't get back to sleep — never can after a skinful the night before — so I went to check what time breakfast was.'

'And did you notice anything odd, at all? Whether Jennifer's door was open or closed?'

'No, nothing. I don't walk past their apartment to get to the reception or breakfast area, so I wouldn't know. Listen, I didn't go anywhere near there, all right?' Ellis said nothing, instead choosing to leave the tension hanging in the air, hoping Ryan might have something to tell him. 'I was gone for a minute or two at most, you can ask Paul. I walked up to reception to see if there was anything on the walls about breakfast, and then came back.'

'We did ask Paul,' Ellis said. 'And he said you were gone for around five minutes.'

Ryan's face went a little redder, this time with anger.

'Well he doesn't know what he's talking about. Why would he say that?'

'I don't know,' Ellis said. 'Why would he?'

'Guilty conscience if you ask me,' Ryan replied. 'He's not exactly an angel himself, let me tell you.'

Ellis leaned in a little closer as Ryan Farley began to explain.

26

The sun beat down on the back of their necks as Hardwick and Flint sauntered through the town of Kakagoustos, the heat feeling like a weight which was being carried. To them at that moment, though, it was nothing compared to the weight of the investigation into the murder of Jennifer Alexander.

The humidity was stifling. Their breathing was laboured and harsh, much like Ellis imagined Jennifer's must have been in the last few moments of her life as the very essence of her being was squeezed from her.

He had reflected on death quite a lot in the past couple of years. Ellis had never really had any real experience of death before he'd met Hardwick, other than having watched his mother die slowly and painfully from bowel cancer a few years previously. His father had left before he was born, and he had never even concerned himself with finding out his name, never mind whether he was still alive or not.

To him, his mother's death had been somewhat expected. The shock of her diagnosis was devastating, but there was always the hope that she'd survive it. On many days, it was more an expectation than a hope. Then, one day, she was gone. But there had always been that chance, and it was diametrically opposed to the sort of death he and Hardwick dealt with. That sort of death was unexpected, unanticipated and usually horrendously violent. It wasn't something which could be explained away with science, nor were you simply one of the statistical victims of disease. To be suddenly and violently taken away from your loved ones was a type of death which Ellis could never really understand.

Hardwick, of course, seemed to be used to it. He didn't know too much about Hardwick's life before he'd met him in the Freemason's Arms in Tollinghill that Friday night two years previously, and each time he had tried to elicit some sort of information, he had been rebuffed. It was clear that Kempston Hardwick was an extremely private person. Perhaps he had skeletons of his own to hide. Perhaps his experiences with death and murder had been more pronounced than Ellis's. It would explain a lot.

Ellis often wondered if Hardwick's cold and emotionless demeanour could ever lead him to kill a man himself, should the need arise. Was there ever a need for murder? He thought not, but it seemed that many disagreed.

He turned his thoughts to the case in hand as it struck him that Hardwick had been one of the last people up and about on the evening Jennifer Alexander died. Surely, if anyone... No. He shook the thought from his mind as quickly as it had entered it.

'I've been speaking to Darryl Potts again,' Ellis said, unable to look directly at Hardwick. 'He told me that Alicia wasn't keen on the idea of coming away with Jennifer and James, mainly because of the bad blood between James and him, but also because Jennifer and James had actually paid for the holiday.'

'What does that have to do with anything?' Hardwick asked.

'Well, apparently Darryl and Alicia have fallen on hard times recently. Alicia used to work as a bank manager in Birmingham, but the bank sold a load of branches after the credit crunch and she was made redundant. Banks aren't exactly hiring people left right and centre at the moment, so she's been a bit stuck. Darryl seemed to think that Alicia felt as though she was some sort of pity case, that she was too proud and wasn't at all comfortable with Jennifer and James paying for them to come away with them.'

'Interesting, but probably not significant, Ellis,' Hardwick replied.

A small dog darted across the road and began yapping at their ankles, a nearby shopkeeper shooing it away with a broom. That the shopkeeper seemed to be the keeper of a shop specialising in kebabs was not a piece of dark humour which was lost on Hardwick. Ellis seemed to barely notice.

They stopped under the awning of a small shop selling newspapers, postcards and beach toys in order to enjoy the shade for a few moments.

'Do you not think pride could cause someone to commit murder?' Ellis asked.

'In exceptional circumstances, perhaps, if the person was severely unhinged. But none of Jennifer's group strike me as that. Besides which, they've all got alibis. We know neither Darryl nor Alicia left the room, plus James was on CCTV all night and was nowhere near the apartment. Add to that the fact that none of them have a motive, and it's looking pretty weak, don't you think?'

'There's always a motive. Couldn't James have done it to collect the life insurance money?' Ellis asked, desperately clutching at straws.

'Jennifer didn't have life insurance, Ellis. James already told us that much. They rented a place together and weren't married, so he wouldn't be entitled to anything anyway. Any murder needs means, motive and opportunity, Ellis, as you well know. James, Darryl and Alicia all had no means, no motive and no opportunity. No, unfortunately that makes it a little bit tricky, because it means that the murderer must be one of the other guests...'

'Well, when I spoke to Ryan Farley, he wasn't at all pleased that Paul had insinuated something about him leaving to check the breakfast times. In fact, he let slip something rather interesting about Paul himself...'

27

Paul Erenson's face was ashen white, the week's sun tan having very quickly disappeared as Hardwick told him what he knew.

At first, his reaction was purely defensive, wanting to know who had told Hardwick what he had just relayed. The panic was clear, the realisation having set in that there was every possibility that this could make him a prime suspect for the murder of Jennifer Alexander.

'Look, I was going through a bad patch, all right? It was a stupid mistake and I've paid the price.'

'All the same, we're going to need the details from you directly, rather than just from a third person,' Hardwick said.

Paul Erenson bowed his head and began to speak. 'It was about four years ago. I was living with my girlfriend at the time, because my parents had kicked me out. She was about two years older than me. I was drunk. I came home and she started some sort of argument about how long I'd been out. The argument got a bit heated and the comments got personal. I just saw red. I started hitting her and the next thing I know I was trying to strangle her with a belt. She pressed charges and I spent twelve weeks inside. Will that do?'

'If it's the truth, yes,' Hardwick said.

'Of course it's the bloody truth! I'm hardly going to admit to something like that if it's not, am I? Look, I did something stupid and I paid the price for it. I'd never been violent before and I've never been violent since. Ryan's just wound up about me saying he left the room — which he did — and is trying to deflect some prying eyes. Can't you even see that?'

Hardwick didn't answer the question, but instead chose to ask his own.

'Why did your parents kick you out, exactly?'

Paul sighed, seemingly having had to tell this story a number of times and not having wanted to revisit it at all.

'It was my dad, mainly. He's of the school of thought that if you haven't got a full-time job by your sixteenth birthday, preferably down the mines, that you're already a failure in life. It's a northern thing. My mum kind of agreed, but got him to accept that these days people tended to go to college, so he shut up for two years and then when I didn't immediately walk out of college in a position to start paying him rent, he kicked me out.'

'Presumably you had to find a job then, though?'

'Well, yeah. Not that I wasn't trying anyway. I had to sleep on a mate's settee for about a month, then I had enough money to rent my own flat for a little while, working three jobs to pay for it. It was just stupid. Then I met Michelle and I moved in with her, which freed things up a bit.'

'Was it a violent relationship?'

'It hadn't been, not until that night. Unfortunately she told the police it had happened loads of times before that. Lying cow. Then I lost two of my jobs and had to start again from scratch. My dad won't talk to me at all — thinks I'm not only a waste of space but a woman beater, and my mum's too ashamed to persuade him otherwise. It was a nightmare trying to get my life back on track again, but I did it. Just one stupid mistake, that was all. It doesn't make me a career criminal or a violent person.'

'Mr Erenson, had you had any falling out with Jennifer Alexander at all?'

Paul took a sip of his drink. 'No, I don't think I ever even spoke to her. Not properly, anyway.'

'But your friend Nick Roder had, hadn't he?'

'Well, yeah, but that's nothing to do with me. He just tried it on with her, I think. No news there, though — he tries it on with everyone.'

'Did he fall out with Jennifer, would you say?'

Paul laughed as he took another sip of his drink. 'No, I wouldn't. I'd say she fell out with him, though. She seemed a bit weird, really. Flaunting it around the pool and wearing low-cut dresses and stuff, giving blokes the come-on. She'd only been here a few hours and had already made a name for herself. But as soon as he approached her the first time around the pool in the afternoon, she was like some sort of ice maiden. Nick thought it was a playing-hard-to-get kind of thing, so he kept having a go. Turns out she wasn't too keen on that.' He laughed again.

'Is Nick a jealous person?' Hardwick asked.

'I dunno really. I think he was kind of surprised, 'cos he tends to get what he wants in that department.

He's pretty good with the birds, is Nick. To be honest, I wasn't paying much attention either way. What was funniest for me was watching Hayley's reaction. That was pure gold.' Seeing Hardwick's raised eyebrow, Paul continued. 'They'd be kind of seeing each other, if you see what I mean. Seeing *to* each other might be a better way to put it. When Nick was trying it on with that Jennifer bird, Hayley wasn't best pleased. Then again, neither was Jennifer's other half, that James bloke.'

As Hardwick concluded their conversation, he noticed the crystal-clear, azure blue swimming pool rippling in the afternoon sun and realised that, for him and this case, nothing was getting clearer at all. In fact, the waters were becoming murkier with every passing minute.

28

Maria Giannakopoulos seemed a little less perturbed by the whole situation than her father did. In fact, she seemed to be capable of showing very little emotion at all, always wearing the same neutral face and seeming like the sort of person who did, rather than the sort of person who felt. When Hardwick and Flint asked her why this was, she seemed to have a rather cathartic response.

'I've been trying to persuade my father to sell the place for years,' she said, in perfect English. 'It's been a long time since the Kollidis made any money. The whole country is dying, and here is no different. I guess now we will have to leave. It is — how you say? — the final nail in the coffin.'

As she spoke, she shuffled piles of paper, sorting various sheets into different piles and folders, although with very little in the way of concentration going into it. It seemed almost like a distraction; an act to look busy. The reception desk was strewn with paper on the side at which Maria was sat, the surface of which was a good two feet lower on her side than it was on the marble counter which the guests had at their chest height.

A computer monitor peered briefly over the top of the marble counter, a number of post-it notes stuck around the edge of the screen. Behind Maria's chair was a series of small pigeonholes, containing either passports or keys — in some cases, both. In short, it looked much like any reception desk in any hotel in any tourist resort in any part of the world.

'Indeed, but there won't be any nails going into any coffins until we've found out who killed Jennifer Alexander,' Hardwick replied.

Ellis Flint, sensing better results from a less direct approach, steered the conversation back towards the personal before Maria could think of a response. 'What do you think your father will do now? If the hotel has to close, I mean.'

'I don't know,' she said, showing the first sign of

emotion since Hardwick and Flint first met her upon checking in at the Kollidis. 'Retire, perhaps. He does not have much money, but it is better to retire now and lose no more, no?'

'But he's been running this place for years. Surely he must have some money put aside,' Hardwick said, like the proverbial bull in a china shop.

Maria went silent for a few moments, seemingly reminded of some painful past memory.

'I think my mother has most of the money, Inspector.'

'Your mother? Where is she?' Ellis asked.

'We do not know. She left ten years ago. Business was still good then, but one day she decided to leave and she has not come back since. I think perhaps my father and her had been arguing many times. I do not know for sure. But the business was good, so it cannot be because of that. Then, one day, we woke up in the morning and she had left.'

'She left? Why?' Ellis asked.

'Promise me you won't say anything to my father. You see, he is not always a pleasant man. When my mother was here, he was a violent man. He used to beat my mother and make her feel terrible. I think this is why she left.'

'Did she say anything before she went?' Hardwick asked, Ellis Flint having been placated into silence.

'No. I did not even see her go. My father woke me up one morning and said to me she had gone during the night.'

Hardwick's eyebrows rose. 'So you didn't see her go? What did she take with her?'

'Nothing. No clothes, no possessions. My father said she took only the money. Since that day, we have had no money. I can see you think this is strange, Inspector. It is true, many people thought this at the time. The police were here, and they gave my father a hard time but in the end they went. They must have believed him.'

Or been unable to prove otherwise, Hardwick thought, as he exchanged glances with Ellis, who, for once, seemed to have cottoned on rather quickly.

29

'Do you not think it rather odd,' Hardwick said as they walked slowly into town, 'that Mrs Giannakopoulos would just disappear without taking any personal belongings at all? Aside from her husband's bank cards, that is.'

'Depends,' Ellis replied. 'If things got a bit heated and she just felt that she had to go. Must happen all the time.'

'I'm sure that story does come up all the time, yes. Bigfoot has been reported hundreds of times, Ellis. Doesn't mean that it's ever true, though. I mean, why would she not even say goodbye to her only daughter? Does that not strike you as a bit odd? In fact, I know it does. I saw the look you gave me in there.'

'What, so you think Stavros was lying to his daughter? And the police?'

'Well, why not? Often it's the simplest explanation which is the correct one, Ellis. Think about it. Perhaps another argument did ensue. Perhaps Stavros did get violent towards his wife again. Perhaps he got so violent, *he killed her*. How do you explain that one away? Simple. You dispose of the body and tell everyone she's walked out on you. A few well-timed cash machine withdrawals to add credence to the story and grab your money before the accounts are frozen should any suspicion arise, and you're home and dry, provided you can keep up the pretence. And let's face it, Stavros Giannakopoulos has proved himself to be a pretty shady character by all accounts. If you'll pardon the pun.'

'What pun?' Ellis asked, oblivious.

'*Accounts*, Ellis. Mr Giannakopoulos said that evening that he needed to go back to his office to work on his accounts, but we've since found out that he was actually... well, reviewing his CCTV footage. Of the sun loungers. And the young ladies on the sun loungers.'

'That doesn't make him a murderer though, does it? Just a bit pervy.'

'Just a bit— Oh, Ellis, come on. That's how these things start. Why do you think the police tend to stop people with the odd brake-light out, or for not indicating at a junction? It's because they'll usually then go on to find out the person has no insurance or is dealing drugs or something. Statistically, those who commit small, minor crimes often do so because they seem insignificant to them based on the bigger ones they commit. It's a fact. And we can only base our investigation on the facts. The problem is, there aren't many facts at the moment.'

'Come on, Kempston. You're always telling me off for letting my imagination run away with me. You know more than most how difficult it is to dispose of a body. Practically impossible, in fact. And in the middle of a bloody tourist resort?'

'We don't know for sure that it was during the tourist season that Mrs Giannakopoulos disappeared, do we? And anyway, *practically* impossible isn't quite impossible. Many people do succeed. Look around you, Ellis. There's the sea, for one. Rowing out in the dead of night and dropping a weighted body as shark food would be a good start. Or there's the dense undergrowth on the edge of the resort. The foxes and wildlife would feast for days. Of course, with this searing heat the best place to leave a dead body is out in the open, as long as you can be sure no-one will spot it. If the body was left uncovered in this heat, it'd decompose in half the time, what with the local animal population helping it along. Then again, things could have stayed closer to home. The Kollidis Beach Hotel stands on quite a bit of its own land. You know, I wouldn't be at all surprised if Mrs Giannakopoulos was buried underneath the bar.'

Ellis Flint narrowed his eyebrows and stayed silent for a few moments, trying to digest all of the information.

'So you think she's dead, then?' he asked, finally.

'Not necessarily, no. Purely conjecture, Ellis. Worth bearing in mind, but I think we're probably better off concentrating on the dead body we *do* know exists for now, don't you?'

* * *

Back at the pool bar, Ellis Flint was trying desperately to compose himself despite all that was going on around him. That was the problem: stuff was going on around him. A murder had been committed, yet everyone was trying to pretend nothing had happened. For some, of course, it was more difficult than other — James had barely been seen, having been mostly comforted by Darryl and Alicia. The atmosphere was a strange mixture of grief, suspicion and hope.

As Ellis shifted uneasily, he noticed that his stool seemed to wobble on the uneven slabs. His eyebrows shot up.

'Kempston!' he hissed. 'Look! The patio slabs aren't even!'

'Ellis,' he replied, without taking his eyes off the newspaper, 'even I'm not quite that obsessive over neatness and order. When have you ever seen a perfectly flat patio? Slabs shift.'

'Yes, especially when there's a decomposing body underneath them!'

Hardwick's eyes rose slowly from the newspaper, not looking at Ellis nor at the patio. Instead, he called out to the barman.

'Arjun, when was this patio laid?'

'Um, when the bar was built. Fifteen years ago, maybe?'

'So it was laid before Mrs Giannakopoulos left?'

'Yes, definitely. I remember them arguing about

how much it cost to build for quite a while before she went.'

Hardwick smiled and returned to his newspaper.

'See, Ellis? Wild theories will get you nowhere.'

'But it was you who—'

'Nowhere, Ellis. Nowhere.'

30

Hardwick stood in the shade between two cream-cladded buildings — a bank and a jeweller's shop — and gazed downward towards the coast. The luscious coarse green grass between the buildings gave way to patches of yellowing burnt areas as the gentle slope careered down towards the sea.

White buildings stood proudly against the shore-line, topped with stunning pink bougainvillaea, as the azure waters licked the golden sands that enjoyed the gentle, carefree weight of the children that played there.

The buildings were indistinguishable and the children little more than ants, dots in the distance. Hardwick liked this view. He liked to observe distant dots, knowing that there was no way that any one of them could see him stood up in the town, relaxing in the shade as he contemplated recent events.

It was in this place that he could properly take everything in, without the glaring sun; the prying eyes of others. With the distance which enabled him to take everything on board.

He ran through the events of the evening in his mind. At 9.45pm Stavros had left the bar, claiming he had to do some work on his accounts, but instead opting to watch back CCTV footage of scantily-clad holidaymakers. Fifteen minutes later, Darryl Potts took Alicia back to her room as she was feeling unwell. At 10.30, Jennifer stormed off back to her room, with James going to check on her around a quarter of an hour later. By 10.50, James had returned to the bar as Jennifer wouldn't let him into the apartment. At this point, then, Jennifer Alexander was still alive.

Nick Roder left the bar around 11.15, with Hayley and Emma going to bed around midnight. Ellis, Ryan and Paul went shortly after. The only other people left had been Hardwick himself and James, who had not left the bar between coming back at 10.50 and the next morning, as the CCTV evidence had proven. The main suspects, then, were Nick, Hayley, Emma, Ryan and Paul. And Ellis.

The possibility was not lost on Hardwick. As much as Ellis was his trusted friend — and he'd never use that word about anyone publicly — his overly logical and fact-based mind just couldn't look past the reality that Ellis was a suspect, with just as much opportunity to murder Jennifer Alexander as anyone. Hardwick was just pleased that he didn't seem to have a motive, thereby knocking him further down the list than most.

Nick Roder had had a motive, though. Being publicly humiliated by Jennifer hadn't best pleased him, and the consumption of alcohol could do remarkable things to a man's brain. That could be said of any of the people that night, though.

As for the other two lads in the group, Paul Erenson had admitted to a history of violence against women, but had no visible reason to kill Jennifer. Ryan Farley, on the other hand, seemed like a fairly quiet, unassuming person but had disappeared for a few minutes — although that was the next morning — for a seemingly spurious reason. And it was the quiet and unassuming ones you had to watch out for.

As far as Hardwick could see, the only motive that either Hayley Saunders or Emma Benson had was that Hayley had been having some sort of holiday romance with Nick, and had witnessed him trying it on with Jennifer that evening. Emma, although she had no motive on the surface of things, did seem unnaturally protective over Hayley.

Ah, yes. And Arjun Beqiri, the Albanian barman. He had been the last man standing at the bar, naturally, as he'd had to lock up at the end of the night. But what reason would he have to kill Jennifer Alexander? True, she had turned down his advances but then she'd had to do so a number of times with a number of different people. One of the downsides to being extraordinarily attractive, Hardwick supposed. And Jennifer was hardly the first holidaymaker Arjun had tried chatting up, and certainly not the first to have rejected him. It just didn't add up.

And then there was the problem of Ellis. The possibility just wouldn't leave Hardwick's mind. It was the drinking. He'd never seen Ellis drink that much in one evening before, and they say you never truly get to know someone until you know them drunk. And Ellis had been *very* drunk. Was this a reason to suspect him, though?

The more Hardwick thought about it, the more the net widened. Whoever killed Jennifer had to be someone she trusted, as all the signs were that she'd opened the door to the apartment and let her killer in. The problem was, she didn't seem to trust anyone. Those with motives, then, had no opportunity. And those with the opportunity, had no motive. That could mean only one thing: Hardwick was missing a vital piece of information.

'Ah, there you are,' Ellis said as he rounded the corner and sidled up alongside Hardwick. 'Admiring the view?'

'Yes, until you frightened the life out of me.'

'Heh. In a world of your own again, were you?'

'Unfortunately so,' Hardwick replied.

'Who was that woman?' Ellis asked, as the pair started to walk back towards the town.

'Hmmm?'

'I saw you about half an hour ago, talking to some Greek-looking woman in the café opposite the market. Just wondered who she was as I don't recognise her from the apartment complex.'

'Oh, just following up on a lead. Tell me, Ellis, do you remember *everything* that happened the night Jennifer Alexander died?'

'What do you mean by everything? If you mean could I have blacked out or forgotten something, no. Why?'

'Oh, just asking.'

31

Hardwick knew that brains generally did the best thinking when they weren't being forced, but instead left to subconsciously mull over the information in the background. It was with this in mind that he had convinced Ellis that it might be a good idea to explore some of the island's culture and heritage, allowing his conscious mind to wander away from the Kollidis Beach Hotel for at least a few hours. Ellis, though, was less than convinced.

'Kempston, we've not got long before most of our suspects will be leaving and heading back to England. And you want to waste the few hours we've got left looking at bits of old pottery?'

'We're not wasting any time, Ellis,' Hardwick

replied. 'What the conscious mind can't figure out, the unconscious mind often can. This is not only a welcome distraction, but a necessary one.'

'In that case, can't we stop everyone leaving? Keep them in the resort, somehow; stop them from going home.'

'And how do you propose we do that, exactly? We already know the police can't be involved, and we've hardly got the power to tell people where they can and can't go. We'll just have to do our best to find out who killed Jennifer Alexander before the flight leaves. And before you say it,' Hardwick said, sensing that Ellis was about to say what he already knew he was going to say, 'No, we wouldn't be better off at the resort. We'd be better off resting our minds with, as you so eloquently put it, some bits of old pottery.'

Ellis was not one to argue with Hardwick's experience of the inner workings of the human mind, no matter how much he failed to see the logic in what he had to say. To him, this was purely a waste of time.

The tour guide, who had introduced himself as Yannis, seemed far keener on the subject of his tour than most other guides Hardwick and Ellis had met. Perhaps he was new to the job, not yet disillusioned by the repetitive nature of having to tell the same stories, over and over again, to the same yet different groups of faceless tourists who either didn't care and just wanted to get back out in the sun or who thought they were showing an interest by asking banal and inane questions.

They were barely three minutes into the tour when Ellis could hardly suppress his chuckle as the first bits of old pottery were shown. Hardwick shot him an icy look which could've frozen the forty-degree Greek sun within seconds.

'This vase, which is pretty complete considering its age, was found by some architects who were building a new housing development on the outside of the town in the 1950s,' the tour guide explained in extraordinarily good English. 'It is quite remarkable in that it shows how the Ancient Greek myths and legends travelled right from the mainland out to the smaller islands, being barely changed on the way. And remember, this was thousands of years ago, so there were no aeroplanes then!'

The assembled tourists laughed far more than they needed to.

'So, when I mention the city of Troy, what comes to mind?'

'Helen and the horse!' a rather keen, plump American woman shouted out, as if there were gold stickers on offer.

'Yes, absolutely. That is by far the most famous legend about Troy, but there is another legend which is much less known, but no less true. That is the story depicted on this vase. Now, in Ancient Greece homosexuality was not considered to be taboo, but instead was a natural means of male sexual pleasure without the need to procreate.'

Hardwick shifted uncomfortably as more and more pairs of eyes from the rest of the group started to move towards them. Ellis, naturally, was oblivious.

'There are a number of different legends which show homosexuality, including the story of Apollo and Hyakinthos. The practice of homosexuality,' the tour guide continued, 'was only condemned much later by Christianity. It was at Troy that Zeus, the great father of the gods, cast his eyes on the handsome Trojan prince Ganymede, whom he stole off the earth by the claws of his eagle, and took to spoil up on Mont Olympos, making him his lover and cup-bearer. It is this image which is depicted on the vase, showing the eagle and the prince.'

'Wasn't Zeus married, though?' a girl of no more than fourteen asked.

'Yes, he was. Very well remembered. Zeus was married to his sister, Hera, who was a very jealous and nasty woman. She was not at all happy about Ganymedes and saw him as a rival for her husband's affections.'

'Erm, what exactly do you mean by "took to spoil"?' one slightly concerned holidaymaker asked.

'That's it!' Hardwick barked. Ellis, what did I tell you? What time is it?'

'Four o'clock.'

'Damn. We need to get back to the resort, and quickly,' he said, dragging Ellis from the tour as the other holidaymakers looked on.

'Can't stop them, can you? One mention of sex and they're off,' the American woman muttered.

32

The taxi driver did as Hardwick said, and drove back to the Kollidis Beach Hotel as quickly as he could.

'Kempston, are you going to tell me what this is all about?' Ellis asked.

'Yes. I think I know who killed Jennifer Alexander.'

'What, because of a vase?'

'Yes, Ellis. Because of a vase. And a flower.'

'Kempston, for crying out loud! Why do you always have to be so cryptic? What flower?'

'Did you not hear the tour guide talking about the story of Apollo and Hyakinthos? Hyakinthos was Apollo's lover. They were in a homosexual relationship. So were Zeus and Ganymede. And Zeus's wife,

Hera, had cottoned on and become jealous and nasty. Don't you see it, Ellis? This is history repeating itself. It's Greek legend being played out again, in Greece! The secretive homosexual relationship, the jealous wife! And Apollo and Hyakinthos, his young lover. Hyakinthos is the Greek word for hyacinth. And who had a picture of a hyacinth on his mobile phone?'

'Darryl Potts!' Ellis exclaimed.

'Yes. Darryl Potts. Our Apollo's young lover.'

Hardwick flung twenty euros at the driver as the cab pulled up outside the Kollidis Beach Resort and clambered out, jogging towards the bar area.

'Arjun, where are Darryl, James and Alicia?'

'Good afternoon to you too, Kempston. I am not sure. Perhaps they have already gone. Would you like a drink?'

'Gone? Gone where?'

'To the airport,' the barman replied.

Before another word was spoken, Hardwick had spun on his heels and jogged back towards the taxi, calling for the driver to wait. Ellis, who had only just reached the bar area and was almost out of breath, groaned noisily as he attempted to follow.

* * *

The journey to the airport was tense, with Hardwick muttering to himself and tapping the sides of his nose with his index fingers as he had wont to do when agitated and "in overdrive", as Ellis liked to call it.

'Is there no quicker way?' Ellis asked the driver, sensing Hardwick's immense discomfort and agitation.

'Quicker? Quicker than the motorway? The motorway which links Kakagoustos and the airport? Hah!' The driver did not even deign to answer the question properly.

Hardwick seemed oblivious to the brief conversation, his brain racing at a million miles an hour as he tried to calculate each of the permutations of what he had suddenly come to realise: that everything they had been led to believe was, in fact, wrong. That James Garfield and Darryl Alexander did not detest each other, but that they had continued the act to throw everyone off the scent that they were, in fact, in a secret relationship. That the odd choice of a picture of a hyacinth on Darryl's iPhone wallpaper had been his own private joke and reminder, that he was Hyakinthos to James's Apollo. That they had, too, been Zeus and Ganymedes, with James ready to pluck

Darryl and sweep him away to their very own Mount Olympos. That Jennifer had found out, or realised what was going on and had become their very own Hera — jealous, nasty and all too powerful in her knowledge. And that was why they had to kill her.

'But *how*, Ellis?' Hardwick asked, as his brain moved on to the logistics of the operation.

'Hmmm?'

'How did they do it? James was on the sun lounger all night, on CCTV. And Darryl was in his apartment all night, as Alicia has testified. She was awake all night as she was so ill.'

'There's only one option, then,' Ellis said. 'That she wasn't killed overnight at all.'

Hardwick snapped out of his psychological stupor. 'Go on.'

'Well, if we're assuming that Darryl and James were the ones who were involved, we also assume that Alicia wasn't and therefore her statements are true. Which means that Darryl couldn't have killed her overnight. And neither could James, as he was on the sun lounger — on CCTV. So therefore Jennifer couldn't have been killed during that time, and it must have been earlier. Alicia said she heard James knocking at the door and some sort of muffled argument which Darryl was witnessing, that Jennifer wouldn't let James into the apartment. Alicia couldn't hear exactly what was said, and she was very ill and disorientated, and we already know that Darryl's witness statement isn't worth the paper it's not even written on, so what if James *wasn't* arguing with Jennifer? What if the knocking had been on *Darryl and Alicia's* door, and that the argument wasn't outside James and Jennifer's door, but theirs, and between Jennifer and Darryl? Suppose Jennifer had decided to confront Darryl that night, and with him having gone back to the apartment earlier she went off to have it out with him. Then the argument that Alicia heard wasn't between James and Jennifer and witnessed by Darryl, but between Darryl and Jennifer.'

Hardwick was silent, mulling over the logistics and permutations of what Ellis was proposing.

'And the argument is ended by Darryl killing Jennifer. James gets back to the apartment just as the deed has been done, and they solidify their account of what they'd say happened. James and Jennifer's apartment would still be open — it was never locked in the first place, as James had never tried to get in. The knocking was Jennifer knocking on Darryl's door.

That's why the door was ajar when I came by in the morning.'

'Ellis. I think you've got it!' Hardwick said, as he pumped his fists in joy. 'My god, Ellis, I could kiss you!'

The taxi driver raised only one eyebrow as he kept his vision firmly on the road ahead.

33

The roads leading up to the airport slowed and slowed until they came to a complete stop with the airport terminal in sight. It was always the way. Airports, the homes of planes, being clogged up with bloody cars.

The queue slewed back towards where Hardwick and Flint's taxi sat, those at the front unloading their passengers and luggage seemingly as slowly as they possibly could, finally causing Hardwick to open the passenger-side door of the taxi, narrowly missing a fast-moving cyclist, before racing around to the back of the taxi and flinging open Ellis's door before he'd even realised what was happening.

'Kempston! We can't just—'

'Yes we can, Ellis. It's quicker than driving. Come on,' Hardwick said as he tugged on Ellis's arm with one hand and threw a bundle of Euros at the driver with the other.

The pair jogged up the side of the road, dodging tourists and suitcases as they made their way to the main airport terminal as quickly as they could, darting into the revolving doors marked *Departures*.

The main terminal building was thronged with people as Hardwick and Flint scanned the crowds as quickly and efficiently as they could to try and find Darryl and James. Everywhere they looked, identikit tourists dressed in shorts and t-shirts lined the tiles, dragging their multi-coloured suitcases behind them, either bronzed or bright red as they grimaced at the thought of having to go back home.

The check-in desks were doing good business in the background, the luggage belts whirring as they whisked people's luggage away to some unknown area at the back of the airport. Coffee kiosks and bureaux de change were busy with their own customers seeking either a caffeine fix or the reas-suring familiarity of the pound sterling. Hardwick had never liked the Euro or its one-size-fits-all approach, denying each of its partner countries their tradition and soul that comes with having its own currency.

All the time, he was on the look out for Darryl Potts and James Garfield. Would Alicia be with them? Or was she also seen as somewhat expendable to Darryl; something which needed to be got rid of? Hardwick had a better idea.

He darted through the thronging crowds, Ellis Flint struggling to keep up with him as his head bobbed about, left, right and centre amongst the countless number of tourists who were all making their ways in different directions. Ellis lost sight of Hardwick for a few moments, before spotting his head popping up from behind a coffee kiosk. He jogged after him, knocking suitcases and small children out of the way as he did so. This was no time for social niceties.

Hardwick reached the airline's information desk at the far end of the concourse and the bespectacled, shy young woman behind the desk looked aghast as the pair pushed through the waiting queue of people and made their way to the front of the desk.

'My name's DI Kempston Hardwick, and this is Ellis Flint. We're from the UK and we're investigating a murder. Can you tell us if Darryl Potts and James Garfield have checked in today, please?'

Ellis, almost imperceptibly, shook his head at Hardwick's slight twisting of the truth. This was a line he'd pulled before, and which, in Hardwick's mind, was perfectly legitimate. He had, after all, technically been born with the full name Dagwood Isambard Kempston Hardwick, although, as he'd once told Ellis, if those were your three names, which one would you choose to use?

'Excuse me!' a bright red and rather large woman shouted. 'But there's a queue here! You can't just go barging around, knocking people out of the way. Who do you think you are?'

'Madam, we are investigating a murder,' Hardwick said, before turning back away from her and whispering to himself: 'Two, if you don't shut up.'

The woman behind the airline information desk tapped the names of Darryl Potts and James Garfield into her computer.

'Jason Garfield... no, I can't see anything,' she said.

'Oh, for— No, not Jason! *James! James* Garfield! This is a murder case, woman!' Hardwick shouted, furious at the time they were losing.

'Sorry,' the woman said, receding into her shell even further. 'No, it is not showing on my computer,' the young woman replied. 'But I can try and—'

'Kempston!' Ellis barked, pointing towards the newsagent's kiosk, where Darryl, James and Alicia were quite casually perusing the selection of magazines on offer, oblivious to the fact that their lives were about to change forever.

34

The crowds seemed to grow and swarm as Hardwick and Flint tried to push their way through to the newsagent's kiosk, desperately trying not to lose sight of Darryl Potts amidst the rabble of tourists who were zig-zagging across their paths.

When they finally made it over to Darryl, James and Alicia, Darryl seemed visibly taken aback at the sight of Hardwick and Flint.

'Darryl, how lovely to see you here,' Hardwick said, panting through his lack of breath.

'Lovely to see you too, Kempston, Ellis. No suitcases with you?'

'Just a flying visit,' Hardwick replied. 'But not of the usual type. Off home today, are you?'

'Yes, our flight leaves in an hour, so we can't hang around. We're going to arrange for Jennifer's body to be flown over on a later flight.'

Hardwick smiled and chuckled a little. 'How do you propose they're going to fly a dead body over, exactly? I mean, yes, if the death had been reported officially and the case had been settled, the Greek authorities would repatriate her body. That would mean informing the police, wouldn't it? And I don't think you really want us to do that, do you?'

Darryl scoffed and made a noise like bus's air brakes. 'And what do you mean by that, exactly?'

'Well,' Hardwick said, cocking his head to one side. 'I'm not entirely sure that the repatriation of Jennifer's body was ever really on your mind. I should imagine you'd be quite happy with her staying in the cold store at the Kollidis, wouldn't you?'

'If you don't mind, Kempston, her fiancé is right here. How can you be so bloody insensitive and say things like that in front of him?'

'Oh, I don't think he's all that bothered, do you. What was the plan? Fly back to England, spin some story about Jennifer staying there? Hope it'd all be lost in the system somewhere along the line? Or did you even think that far ahead? Because this whole week has been one huge catastrophic mess. No plans, no strategy. Just a hodgepodge of circumstances and cracks which you'd managed to plaster over very quickly. You see, we thought we were after some sort of criminal mastermind, but we were wrong.'

'Are you drunk, Kempston?' Alicia asked, still not having cottoned on to what Hardwick was saying.

'Ah, yes. Alicia. And what were you going to do with her? I mean, you couldn't exactly have her running around England telling everyone that Jennifer was dead, could you? But she couldn't just disappear as well, wiped off the face of the earth as if she didn't exist. Was anything planned at all? Or were you just hoping another hastily-hatched plan would fall into place?'

Alicia spoke again. 'Are you trying to say that—'

'Oh, yes. I am. It was your boyfriend who killed Jennifer. It wasn't James banging on Jennifer's door, but Jennifer banging on Darryl's door — your door. When Darryl went to "see what was going on", Jennifer was outside confronting him. That's when he ended up killing her, just as James got back from the bar and they hatched the plan to cover it up, being the perfect alibis for each other due to their apparently hating each other, with you as the third alibi. Quite clever for an on-the-spot plan, I must admit.'

'But... I don't— Confronting him about what?' Alicia asked, looking suspiciously at Darryl and James as she spoke.

'About the fact that your boyfriend and James have been having a secret affair, Alicia. About the fact that Jennifer had found out and was going to expose them. When you heard Jennifer telling James that she felt embarrassed and ashamed, she was talking to Darryl. She wasn't embarrassed and ashamed that James had left her to be chatted up by Nick Roder, but that Darryl and James had made a fool of her by carrying on behind her back. So what was the plan?' Hardwick said, turning to Darryl and James. 'If there was a plan, that is. Was Alicia going to be next?'

A sob came from Alicia's mouth as her hand rose to subdue it. 'Darryl... Tell me it's not true. Please!'

Before an answer came, Darryl had hot-footed it off towards the terminal doors, up-ending a stand full of newspapers as he went. Hardwick darted after him almost as quickly, as the pair headed for the exit.

Another push through the growing crowds of

tourists ensued before Hardwick finally got out of the terminal doors, the sun beating down on him once again as he saw Darryl Potts bounce off the bonnet of the braking taxi.

35

'I feel so stupid!' Alicia said, as she sobbed into her hands, her and Hardwick sat in the cold, soulless room at the airport. 'They say you can always tell, don't they? How did I not see it?'

Hardwick, who had not one shred of romantic understanding in his being, tried to be as poignant and prophetic as possible.

'You were blinded. Perhaps you did see it. But if it's not something you want to see or believe in, your mind won't let you see it. We're all blind to our own minds.'

The door opened and Ellis came in, accompanied by the airport manager who had brought a pot of tea.

After Darryl had been handily stopped in his

tracks by a ton of metal, he had been detained by Hardwick and a security guard until the police and ambulance service had been called. Ellis, meanwhile, had stayed with James and Alicia, the security team in the airport having been on the scene pretty quickly after the commotion was noticed.

As far as Hardwick was concerned, his week had been a success: he'd finally seen evidence of some uncharacteristic Greek efficiency. The airport staff, once Ellis had told them what had happened, were more than accommodating, having shuffled him and Alicia off into a side room whilst the security staff detained James until the police arrived.

'I spoke to the ambulance crew,' Ellis said. 'It looks as though Darryl's going to survive. The police are waiting to speak to him as well. They've arrested James. They'll probably want to speak to you too, Alicia.'

'But what can I say? I don't know anything. I only found out myself five minutes ago!'

'I know, but Ellis and I will do all we can to help,' Hardwick said. 'From what I saw, James looked just about ready to admit to everything. Now the police are involved, they can use DNA evidence and all sorts of things to prove it. All you have to do is tell them your version of events.'

'I... I don't even know what's real any more. I just feel so sorry for Jennifer. I mean, not only was she murdered but it wasn't even her fault. The only thing she did wrong was to find out the truth.'

'Sometimes the truth can be far more dangerous than fiction,' Hardwick said. 'There's a lot to be said for living in your own dreamworld.'

It was at that point that the door to the side room flew open and two burly, very Greek-looking police officers entered.

'You are Mr Hardwick, yes?' the older and sweatier of the two said.

'Yes, that's correct,' Hardwick said, with his hand extended and a proud smile plastered across his face.

'And this is Mr Flint?'

'That's right, yes. I suppose you want me to explain how we worked it all out?'

'No, I want you to come with me. We are arresting you both. We would like to speak to you about why you seem to have obstructed justice and interfered with a crime scene.' He turned to his younger colleague. 'Put handcuffs on them both.'

36

Greek prison cells weren't much more pleasant than those at Tollinghill Police Station, where Hardwick had once found himself for a similar case of getting in the way of police officers. That time it was DI Rob Warner of Tollinghill Police, who had taken exception to Hardwick's interference, as he saw it. With Hardwick later having solved the murder, Warner's temperament softened somewhat.

Since then, Warner had called on Hardwick specifically to help solve the murder of a famous psychic medium. He'd had to grovel to make up for the way he had treated Hardwick — a memory which Hardwick was often keen to recall when in the DI's presence.

'Obstructing justice?' Ellis said, still not quite believing his situation. 'It's mad. I told you we should have told the police from the start!'

'No, Ellis, you didn't. I did. You convinced me to take on the investigation. Anyway, we didn't obstruct justice; we facilitated it. The police officers here will realise that soon enough and will have to let us go.'

'And what if they don't? We'll be banged up here for god knows how long, trying to deal with a justice system we aren't familiar with and a jail sentence we can only guess at. Mrs F will go loopy.'

'She needn't know, Ellis. I'm sure we'll be out of here before long. We can just tell her our flight was delayed, or we got to the airport late.'

'Late? Kempston Hardwick, late? She'll never believe that for a second.'

'Don't panic, Ellis. We'll sort something out.'

Ellis sighed and paced the cell for the hundredth time. It was only thanks to the overcrowding of prison cells in the drink-and-drug-induced resort of Kakagoustos that Hardwick and Flint were forced to share a cell.

'Realistically, Kempston, how long are we likely to be in here?'

'Not long.'

'Not long? Don't lie to me, Kempston. I know you know about things like this. What are we looking at?' Ellis said, closing in on Hardwick.

'Well, it depends if they decide to take it to trial. If they do, the maximum period of detention before a trial is eighteen months.'

'Eighteen months?!' Ellis screamed. 'How many bloody planes are we supposed to have missed?!'

'It's purely academic, Ellis,' Hardwick said, not raising his voice or showing any signs of concern whatsoever. 'We're EU citizens, and as such are entitled to phone a family member back home to notify them of our arrests.'

'What? You didn't—'

'No, I did not phone your wife, Ellis. I'm not an imbecile, nor do I have a death wish. I may have told a little white lie and said that I was phoning a family member, but instead I called DI Warner.'

'Kempston, you bloody genius! Do you reckon he'll be able to pull a few strings?'

'I should imagine so. He owes us a favour, anyway. I should imagine he'll probably embellish our track records with this sort of thing. Either that or he'll have to make some sort of assurances that we'll be dealt with in the UK instead. Maybe make out that we're wanted for bigger things there. Either way, you'll be picking post-it notes off the cupboard doors before you can say "Yes, Mrs Flint".'

'Oh God,' Ellis said, his hands shooting up to his mouth. 'What about Stavros? If the police are involved, he'll lose everything, won't he?'

'I don't think so, no, Ellis. In fact, I'm pretty sure he'll be absolutely fine from now on.'

Barely ten minutes later, the door to the cell was unlocked and the younger of the two police officers stood to let Hardwick and Flint out.

'It seems you have friends in high places,' the officer said.

With Maria out in the town picking up some groceries, Stavros was manning the reception at the Kollidis Beach Hotel, his head rested on his hand as he played Solitaire on the reception computer.

The woman walked in quietly but purposefully, her suitcase trundling behind her as she approached the reception desk. Stavros, though, was in no mood for walk-ins. Check-in day was once a week, and that was that. He dealt with holiday companies only, not bloody backpackers.

'Sorry, no walk-ins. The sign on the door says so,' he said, not taking his eyes from the deck which he'd just clicked to turn over. Sodding nine of hearts was second in the pile. He needed that one. Just his luck.

And that bloody woman was still standing there. Perhaps he'd been a bit rude. Perhaps she wasn't a walk-in after all. Perhaps she just wanted the key to her room. Right now, he didn't care for people one bit. He was in another place entirely.

'OK, which room?' he asked, his eyes still not leaving the computer screen.

The woman removed her sunglasses and ran her fingers through her short, dark hair.

'The bedroom,' she replied.

At the sound of her voice, Stavros finally took his eyes off the screen and looked up at her.

It had been ten years, but she hadn't aged a bit.

MORE BOOKS BY ADAM CROFT

RUTLAND CRIME SERIES

1. What Lies Beneath
2. On Borrowed Time
3. In Cold Blood

KNIGHT & CULVERHOUSE CRIME THRILLERS

1. Too Close for Comfort
2. Guilty as Sin
3. Jack Be Nimble
4. Rough Justice
5. In Too Deep
6. In The Name of the Father
7. With A Vengeance
8. Dead & Buried
9. In Too Deep
10. Snakes & Ladders

PSYCHOLOGICAL THRILLERS

- Her Last Tomorrow
- Only The Truth
- In Her Image
- Tell Me I'm Wrong
- The Perfect Lie
- Closer To You

KEMPSTON HARDWICK MYSTERIES

1. Exit Stage Left
2. The Westerlea House Mystery
3. Death Under the Sun
4. The Thirteenth Room
5. The Wrong Man

All titles are available to order from all good book shops.

Signed and personalised books available at
adamcroft.net/shop

EBOOK-ONLY SHORT STORIES

- Gone
- The Harder They Fall
- Love You To Death
- The Defender

To find out more, visit adamcroft.net

**Kempston Hardwick and Ellis Flint
return in**

THE THIRTEENTH ROOM

OUT NOW

**Over two weeks, three guests enter Room 13
at the Manor Hotel, but none comes out
alive...**

When a married man seemingly kills himself at a local
hotel, Kempston Hardwick is not so sure the death was
suicide.

As he tries to convince the police to investigate, Kempston yet again throws himself into an investigation
where all is not as it seems, but not before the Manor
Hotel is home to more suspicious deaths...

Turn the page to read the first chapter...

THE THIRTEENTH ROOM
CHAPTER 1

Elliot Carr closed his eyes and turned his head upwards as he tried to blot out the inevitable argument which had ensued. They could never go anywhere — anywhere — without some sort of drama from Scarlett.

He'd known she was a drama queen when he'd first met her, but that was one of things that had first attracted him to her. It was certainly far less irritating than that erroneous extra 't' at the end of her name, which her parents had added in order to make her name 'unique' and 'different'. Everything her parents had ever done had been unique and different, so why would they stop at naming their child?

If the truth be told, it was Scarlett's parents he disliked. Sure, Scarlett had her pretensions, her airs and graces, but she couldn't be blamed for them. It was purely down to her parents, who'd led her to believe that she had some sort of divine right over other people just because her father was a banker and her mother had delusions of being a successful novelist. Elliot had always tried to stifle the laughter when Irma told people she was a full-time writer. Sure, she spent all of her time writing, but she'd never earned a penny from it. That didn't bother her. She didn't need to, what with Robert raking home in a week what most people could only hope to earn in a year.

Where Elliot came from, money didn't make someone a better person. In fact, he found that the opposite was usually true. His more modest upbringing though, had brought with it a certain talent for tact and tongue-biting, which was serving him well now as Scarlett launched into another tirade.

'This is meant to be our *anniversary*, Elliot!' she yelled, emphasising the occasion as if he could have somehow forgotten.

'Yes, I know it is. But you can hardly blame me for the traffic problems, Scarlett. Or the car breaking down. Or the mix-up with the hotel room.'

'How am I supposed to know it wasn't you who mixed up the rooms?' she asked, wrenching a phone charger from her suitcase and throwing it down on the bed. 'After all, it was you who booked it.'

Yes, because I'm the one who always does these things, Elliot thought. *Maybe if you got off your privileged backside and—* 'The receptionist said it was to do with their new computer system. Just one of those things.'

'Just one of those things,' Scarlett repeated, with mock laughter. 'Just like the car breaking down. Again.'

'And what do you want me to do about it now?' Elliot asked, trying desperately to keep a lid on his temper. 'It's been back in to the dealership three times now and they've said they can't find a fault.'

'Well maybe if we'd gone for the Mercedes instead, like I wanted, then we wouldn't have to keep taking it back to the bloody dealership, would we?' she replied, tugging her make-up bag loose from under Elliot's neatly folded shirts.

Elliot sighed. There was no point. They'd been over this a hundred times before. How, in fact, it was he who'd wanted the Mercedes but Scarlett had twisted his arm into buying the BMW. How he'd pointed out that the Mercedes would be more reliable but that Scarlett had preferred the interior on the BMW. How she was always bloody right, even when she was wrong.

'Is that it?' she said, thrusting her hands on her hips. 'A sigh?'

'What do you want me to say?' Elliot asked, hoping for some sort of tip as to how he could end this daft charade. After five years of marriage, though, he knew there was only one way.

'Nothing. There's nothing you can say.'

'Right. Well I'm going to the bar, then.'

***

'Large scotch, please,' Elliot said, the barman's permanent smile putting him on edge. He was never sure how to react when people were overly nice. Should he drop his defences and smile back, no matter how upset or annoyed he was, or should he allow it to infuriate him even more to the point where he wanted to punch him in the face? *Rise above it*, he told himself. He wasn't angry at the barman; he was angry at Scarlett.

He was amazed at how often he had to tell himself that. As far as he was concerned, it just went to show that Scarlett's attitude and behaviour had permeated every fibre of his being and was starting to affect so many different areas of his life. He wasn't one for confrontation, though, and preferred to keep things bottled up. That wasn't a problem, as he never stayed angry for long. At some point tonight he'd have calmed down, Scarlett would have just pretended the whole thing never happened, she'd flounce down to dinner, they'd have a bottle or two of wine, head back upstairs and... Well, she had her uses.

Right now, though, his attention was fixed firmly on the glass of scotch, for no other reason than to take his mind of the fact that he'd just paid twelve pounds for it. *Way to calm a man down*, he thought.

He sloshed the amber liquid around in his glass, clinking the ice off the side of the glass as it slowly melted, releasing the potent fumes of the whisky.

'Long day?' the barman asked as he wiped between the beer pumps with a cloth.

'Hmm? Oh. No, sorry,' Elliot said, waking himself from his stupor. 'Silly argument with my wife. Just one of those things.'

'Ah. I did wonder,' he said. 'Not often you get men drinking scotch at six o'clock in the evening.'

'No. Well, it'll be my only one, I suppose. Especially at these prices.'

The barman laughed a knowing laugh, as if he'd heard that line a few times before. 'Funny. You don't seem like the marrying type to me,' he said.

Elliot allowed himself to smile for the first time that evening. 'No. I'm starting to think that might be the case myself.'

The comfort of the Freemason's Arms seemed like luxury to Ellis Flint. He was a firm believer that holidays were meant to be relaxing affairs, but the one he'd just returned from had been anything but.

'You two are bloody murder magnets from what I hear,' the landlord, Doug Lilley, said as he pulled on the pump to pour Ellis's pint. 'In fact, perhaps it's in my best interests that I bar you,' he added, laughing.

'I think you're safe,' Ellis said. 'Lightning never strikes twice.' Indeed, the very first murder that Ellis and his friend Kempston Hardwick had investigated had taken place in the Freemason's Arms a little over three years earlier.

'Bloody strikes constantly when you two are about,' Doug replied. 'Rate you're going, you'll turn this place into some sort of cheap detective series location.'

'Well, at least we're doing our bit for the community. I can't see them closing down the police station if the murder rate stays this high.'

Tollinghill Police Station had been earmarked for closure by the county force in the previous few months as part of the present government's cost-cutting exercises. It was all about 'streamlining' and 'centralising services'. Once all of the corporate-speak had been cut through, the bottom line was that it came down to money. Liberty and safety had been reduced to mere commodities.

'Heh. Every cloud and all that,' Doug said, leaning in towards Ellis. 'Here, that reminds me. Did you hear about that bloke topping himself down at the Manor Hotel in South Heath last Thursday?'

'No,' Ellis said. 'What happened?'

'Hung himself from the rafters on the top floor. Nothing suspicious, like. Well, not officially, anyway. But it's a bit weird, ain't it, after all them stories about the ghosts and that?'

'Ghosts?' Ellis asked, his interest piqued. Ellis's interest in the paranormal had come to the fore on more than one occasion recently, and he was sure that many of the odd goings on in and around Tollinghill could be attributed to supernatural forces. He vaguely recalled a ghost story concerning the Manor Hotel but couldn't remember any details.

'Yeah, an old woman supposedly haunts it,' Doug said. 'Story goes, a child died there, back when it was a private manor, back in Victorian times. They reckon it was the nanny who had poisoned the young lad, and they sacked her on the spot even though she said she didn't do it. Few years later, the old dear dies in poverty and never got to clear her name. Legend has it that it's her ghost who still haunts the manor, trying to protest her innocence.'

Ellis felt the hairs on the back of his neck stand up and realised his breathing was becoming more and more shallow.

'Apparently it all kicked off when they converted it into a hotel,' Doug continued. 'The builders had been doing some renovation work and took some tiles off the roof. Turns out there was a secret hidden room on the top level, which no-one knew about. They reckon it's what would've been the servants' quarters. The room where the nanny would've lived. That's when it all started kicking off.'

'Kicking off?' Ellis asked.

'Well, they gradually turned the top floor rooms into more hotel rooms, as well as keeping a couple for the staff. Housekeepers and that. Few weeks later, people started seeing things. Couple of people reckon they saw an old woman sat at the end of their bed, crying. Quite a lot of footsteps coming from the room where she would've lived, too.'

'Sounds like a nice little bit of marketing to me,' Ellis said, not believing his own cynicism but trying desperately to come up with a rational explanation in order to stop himself getting completely spooked.

'That's where you're wrong, see. The hotel owners went and spoke to a couple of the families who lived there, back when it was in private hands. Turns out the previous owner said his mum used to hear someone knocking on her bedroom door at night, even if she was the only person there. And other people saw things, too.'

Ellis sat back and thought for a moment. 'Doug,' he said, leaning forward once more. 'What's this got to do with this bloke's suicide, exactly?'

'You tell me, Ellis,' Doug said, standing up and brushing down the bar with a cloth. 'You tell me.'

Want to read on?

Visit adamcroft.net/book/the-thirteenth-room/ to grab your copy.

ACKNOWLEDGMENTS

To Joanne, Claire and my mum for being my beta readers once more and pointing out the blazingly obvious errors which I inevitably make.

Extra thanks to Joanne for having actually ensured this book ever got written, mainly by helping to plug the enormous plot holes which I couldn't work myself out of on my own.

To Sean Caruana Webster for his fascinating, insightful and invaluable knowledge of Greek mythology and symbolism.

To Barry and Rick for their superior knowledge and assistance in levels of grammar pedantry of which even I am incapable.

To David Lovesy, my superb cover designer who is simply a design god.

To Astrid and the rest of the team at Literature & Latte who very kindly gave me a copy of their wonderful Scrivener software, which made putting this book together much easier than it was proving up until that point.

To Bob, who first brought Kempston to life and made him so much easier to write. The very best actors take a character and mould them with their own take, but Bob's not bad either.

Without these people, this book would not ever have been possible. So blame them.

Any remaining errors, omissions, spelling mistakes or cock-ups are entirely my fault. I accept no liability for coffee rings or paper cuts.